Deceitful Intentions

Charleen A. Williams
Allison M. Whitmore

Copyright©

Dedication

Charleen A Williams - *Nothing happens in my life without God! This book is a different kind of accomplishment! I'm used to sitting at my computer and writing based on my own thoughts and accord. With this novel, God entrusted someone else to help me get this story done. I am forever thankful for my friend and co-author Mrs. Allison Whitmore. I could not have done this without your unique voice and vision. In thanking Allison I must also thank her husband and our editor Eric Whitmore, for his contributes to this story. I appreciate you both always.*

This goes without saying, but I'll say it anyway! My husband and my children are my biggest cheerleaders. They support me in every endeavor I take on. I want to thank them for always being my support system and weathering my storms as I get through every story I tell. I do this for you all! I love y'all.

Allison M. Whitmore - *First, I want to thank my Heavenly Father because I don't and can't do anything without him. In the beginning, writing this book was a challenge for me. I wanted to make sure that I did not compromise my beliefs; with that being said, I enjoyed writing this book with my co-author and friend, Charleen Williams. I want to thank her for being open to the vision that God gave me for the book.*

Thank you to my husband, Eric, for always being there and sharing your ideas for the book. I love you always. To my children, Rahsaan, Sharnell, Eric Jr., and Allera, always remember what God said about you. Dad and I love you. Malani, my favorite granddaughter (my only grandchild), you are my legacy! You will do great things. Pop pop and I love you.

Thank you to my village that God created, who loves, prays, encourages, corrects, and supports me always. Love you all.

Table of Contents

EPILOGUE: Two Years Later
The Next Morning - Crestwood Correctional Facility

Introduction
A Storm of Emotion

The evening had settled into an uneasy stillness inside the Alexanders' home. Brian sat on one side of the bed, his head in his hands, while Morghan stood by the dresser, her back turned to him. The space between them felt heavy, filled with a mix of grief, confusion, and something darker that neither of them wanted to acknowledge.

The loss of their daughter, Amiya Reign, had shattered their world. In the weeks since her passing, the cracks in their relationship had deepened, and now those cracks were threatening to split wide open. The air between them crackled with tension, as if they were both standing on the edge of a cliff, waiting to see who would fall first.

Morghan's eyes were red and swollen from hours of crying, and her shoulders slumped with the weight of it all. She began to walk toward the door, desperate to escape the conversation she knew was coming—one she had been avoiding for days.

Brian's voice cut through the silence before she could reach the handle. "Why do you spend so much time with Tabitha?" His words were low, but the frustration in his voice was impossible to miss. "I get that you need support, but it feels like you're relying on her more than me."

Morghan froze, her hand hovering over the doorknob. She didn't turn to face him, but her body tensed as his words sank in. She knew this conversation was coming. Brian had been watching her closely every time she mentioned Tabitha's name, every time she came home later than she had planned.

"Tabitha understands me, Brian." Morghan's voice trembled, but there was an edge of defense in her tone. She turned slowly, her eyes meeting his. "She knows what it's like to lose a child. She's been through this pain, this heartache. I can't expect you to understand it the way she does."

Brian's jaw tightened, and he ran a hand through his hair in frustration. "I'm not saying you shouldn't have support, Morghan. I'm trying to be there for you, but lately... it feels like she's more than just a friend. Like you're turning to her instead of me."

Morghan's eyes widened, disbelief flashing across her face. "Are you serious? What exactly are you accusing me of?" You were the one who suggested I go to the grief meetings. That's where I met her, remember? What exactly are you accusing me of?"

"I don't know," Brian said, his voice rising with a mix of desperation and hurt. "It's just the way you talk about her, the way you light up when you mention her. It's like you're finding comfort in her arms instead of mine. And I suggested we go, you decided to go alone."

"Brian, how can you say that?" Morghan's voice cracked, her frustration boiling over. "I love you. But you can't possibly understand what this feels like, not the way she does. We've bonded over our grief, and I need that right now."

"And what about me?" Brian shot back, his eyes glistening with unspoken pain. "Amiya was my daughter too. I'm grieving her just as much as you are. But I feel like I'm losing you, Morghan. Like you're pushing me away, and I'm standing here with my hands tied, watching you drift further into someone else's world."

Morghan's tears flowed freely now, the weight of his words breaking through her defenses. "I'm not replacing you, Brian. I'm just... I'm trying to survive. I need you, but I also need someone who truly knows this kind of pain. Tabitha gets it in a way no one else can."

Brian's anger softened, replaced by a deep sadness. He reached out, taking her trembling hand in his. "I'm sorry, Morghan. I know I haven't been able to be what you need. But I'm still here. I want to help you through this in my own way. Let me be the one you turn to. We can figure this out together."

Morghan nodded, though the pull to be with Tabitha still lingered at the edges of her mind. She kissed Brian gently, a soft promise she wasn't sure she could fully keep. "I won't be late," she whispered, grabbing her purse from the dresser.

Brian watched her walk toward the door, a pit forming in his stomach as she left. He could feel her slipping further away into Tabitha's world—one he didn't understand and wasn't sure he wanted to.

As the door clicked shut behind her, the silence in the house deepened, and Brian sat back on the bed, alone with his thoughts, wondering how much more he could take.

Chapter One
The Beginning of the End

The sun shined brightly over the small town of Frisco Texas, casting a warm glow on the gathered mourners. The air was heavy with grief as the church filled with family and friends of Amiya Reign Alexander. Brian and Morghan stood side by side at the funeral of their beloved 8-year-old daughter, who lost her battle with Sickle Cell. Her body was a little frail but dressed in pink and white pajamas. There seemed to be a little smile on her face as she lay in the rose-colored casket surrounded by beautiful flower arrangements. She was finally pain-free. Amiya fought a courageous battle against sickle cell disease, but her fragile body could no longer withstand its relentless grip. The community rallied around the Alexanders, offering support and prayers during Amiya Reign's difficult journey. Now, they stood together, their hearts heavy with sorrow, bidding farewell to their precious child. The church was filled with white lilies, symbolizing purity and peace. The pews were filled with tearful faces, friends, family, and neighbors, all united in their grief and love for Amiya Reign.

As the pastor's voice resonated with compassion, the couple clung to each other, finding solace in their shared sorrow. Brian, a strong and resilient man, fought to hold back tears that threatened to betray his stoic façade. Morghan, a pillar of strength for her family, struggled to find words to express the depth of her pain. They stood together with hearts heavy and filled with sorrow as they said goodbye to their one and only daughter.

As the service began, Morghan and Brian were flooded with memories of Amiya's infectious laughter and bright smile. She had an unwavering spirit to fight this disease from the beginning. Amiya's journey was remarkable and would never be forgotten. Her parents would make sure of that.

As the service came to an end, Morghan and Brian clung to one another tightly, trying to find strength in their shared pain. One thing was quite certain in the midst of this turmoil. And it was that their lives would never be the same without Amiya Reign.

In the days that followed, Morghan and Brian sought comfort in the memories they had created with their daughter. They looked at pictures and watched videos of her as a baby and beyond. They fought extremely hard to avoid the grief pain, but each day got harder and harder to cope with the void they were missing so much in their heart and home. There was a great silence that fell over the unusually somber home. Morghan had barely gotten out of bed since returning from the grave site she visited each day since the funeral until recently when she just stopped going. Brian trying everything possible to control his grief and still be there for Morghan was beginning to weigh heavy on him.

"Hey babe, Brian called out as he entered the dark bedroom. The sun was shining bright outside, but the blackout curtains were completely closed as if it was night. Do you want to go out and get some lunch?"

"No, Brian, I'm actually not hungry right now."

"Morghan, you have to eat and get out of this room. It's not healthy for you to consistently lay in bed all day. Let's go get some sunshine and some food. I'm sure it will make you feel a little better."

"I'm not ready to go back outside right now. I miss my daughter, and no amount of food or sunshine's going to change that. Just leave me alone, please!"

Feeling defeated once again, Brian calmly closed the door to let her be. It was obvious that Morghan was falling into a deep depression, but Brian had no idea how to fix it.

Brian sat at the kitchen table filled with concern as he watched his wife Morghan move through the motions of daily life. It had been weeks since they said their heartbreaking goodbyes to their beloved daughter, Amiya Reign. Yet, the weight of grief still hung heavy in the air. Brian could see that Morghan was struggling to find her footing in the world without their daughter, but he was determined to be her rock, her source of strength and comfort. Brian was determined to help his wife get better.

The next morning, Brian got up out of bed and pulled the curtains back without waiting for Morghan's approval.

"Rise and shine, babe! It's a new day."

"Really, Brian?" Morghan replied as she pulled the covers further over her head.

"Babe, come on, get up! I'll meet you downstairs. I'm off all day today, so we're spending the day together. Get up!" Brian went into the bathroom to start the shower for Morghan. She always waited for the bathroom to get steamy before she would go in to take her shower.

"Come on bae, get up. I'll meet you in the kitchen in 15 minutes. Please don't make me come back in here." Brian warned Morghan before closing the bedroom door. Against her wishes, Morghan slowly moved the covers off her face and began to crawl out of bed slowly. Her eyes squinted against the bright sunshine as she sat up on the edge of the bed, moving her feet around in search of her red fluffy slippers. Although she knew Brian was right about her needing to get out, she still didn't totally agree with it. None the less, she obeyed her husband's wishes and went to take a shower so she could meet him in the kitchen. The warm water felt like heaven as Morghan stood in the shower, allowing it to run across her face and body. She fought back flashes of Amiya as she wanted to get through her shower without breaking down.

"Bae are you ok in there?" She heard Brian calling out to her as he knocked on the door. Bae, it's been 30 minutes." Morghan, unaware of the time that had lapsed sent she stepped into the shower, called out, and replied.

"Yes, Brian, I'm fine! I'll be out in a minute."

"Ok!" Morghan got out of the shower and stood in the mirror staring at herself. She hadn't really been eating since

Amiya's health had taken a turn for the worse, and it was certainly showing. Her face had thinned out a little more than she was used to. Her hourglass shape, which her husband loved so much, had transformed into more of a flute shape. The curves had disappeared along with the natural apple bottom she had worked so hard to build. At that moment, she realized it was not going to come back if she didn't get it together. Before Amiya's illness got bad, Morghan was in the gym daily with Brian, working out to keep their bodies in shape. It had been months since they went anywhere near a gym or worked out. This was completely unacceptable in her mind.

"Morghan, what have you done?" She thought to herself as she rambled through the closet, trying to find something that could still fit her thin body. She came across a blue and white maxi sundress that was a little big, but it would hide the big weight change for the moment. Moghan put on the dress and slid into her clear Marc Jacob sandals, fixed her bob-length hair, added a little makeup to enhance her caramel-colored skin tone, and headed to the kitchen to meet Brian.

"Tada," Morghan announced as she entered the kitchen. Brian turned in disbelief, as he had not seen his wife in anything other than his baggy gray or black sweatpants and a t-shirt for months.

"Beautiful babe," he whispered as he kissed her on the cheek. Morghan took a seat on the stool at the counter as Brian poured her a cup of tea. She noticed a pamphlet on the countertop. What's this, Brian she asked as she pulled it closer. Oh, that's a flyer for a program I thought you might be interested in. Grief counseling? Well, I thought it might help us to deal with our loss a little better. I'm willing to go to some meetings also if you want to try it. Morghan was silent for a moment as she read over the flyer. No, this may be good for me. Why just you? Brian seemed a little confused. Well, you seem to be doing okay! I may just go alone to see if it helps. Do you mind? Umm, I guess it'll be ok. I was thinking it could help us both, but ok. There's actually a meeting later today; if you would like to go, I can drop you off and come back to get you after. With a short sigh, Morghan agreed to go to the grief meeting.

Chapter Two
A Bond Built of Shared Grief

Morghan walked into the small meeting room, her heart heavy with sorrow and a slight gleam of hope. This had been her fourth meeting since Brian gave her the pamphlet. It had been a little over three months since she lost her daughter Amiya Reign, and attending the grief meetings had become a vital part of her healing journey. As she took her seat, she glanced around the room, meeting the eyes of fellow mourners who understood the depths of her pain.

In the corner of the room, Morghan noticed a newcomer to the meeting. She had never seen her attend before. There was a sadness in her eyes that mirrored Morghan's pain, but there was also an undeniable trace of strength and resilience that she carried also. Morgan instantly felt an unexplainable connection to the woman without even knowing her name. It was as if their souls had recognized each other's pain and sought out solace in a shared understanding.

After the meeting, Morghan mustard up the courage to approach the women.

"Hi, I'm Morghan," she said softly, her voice laced with vulnerability. The woman looked up, her eyes filled with a mixture of grief and curiosity.

"I'm Tabitha, she replied. I don't think I've seen you here before Tabitha, are you new? Yes, well no, this is my first meeting in a while. Not quite what I remember, though."

"How do you mean? Morghan asked.

"I'm not sure, actually, but it's nothing like what I experienced the last go round. Everyone was so open and willing to share."

"Yea, I see what you mean; they are all welcoming." As they began to talk, Morghan and Tabitha realized just how much they had in common. Both had experienced the devastation of losing a child. They had endured the same sleepless nights and the same heart-wrenching goodbyes. Their shared experiences created an immediate bond, a sense of understanding that only those who had walked a similar path could truly grasp.

In the weeks that followed, Morghan and Tabitha spent hours together sharing their stories, their tears, and their hopes for the future. They discovered that their grief journey was unique, yet intertwined. They found comfort in the simple act of being seen and heard by someone who had experienced the same loss firsthand. Tabitha had not only lost her son, but she had also lost her husband in that terrible car accident.

"Tabitha, I don't know how you've been able to maneuver through this ordeal. I was barely making it with the loss of Amaya; you've lost Jerrimi Jr and Jerrimi Sr.

"Yeah, I don't know either, Morghan! I'm thankful to have met you, though. Being new to this state and not having anyone here for support was extremely hard. But I knew I was not going back to Louisiana. There are too many memories there. We were moving here to start a new life, so I made a promise to my husband and son to continue with that plan. It hasn't been easy, but I'm getting better each day. And now that we have each other to lean on, that makes it even better."

"Cheers to new friends! Morghan replied as they toasted their afternoon margaritas while waiting on the waiter to bring the lunch they ordered.

After lunch, Morghan and Tabitha parted ways for the day.

"Listen Morghan, if you're not busy with Brian later, you can come around and hang out if you want. That sounds fun, Tabitha! I will give you a call if it's a go! I don't want to speak before talking to Brian. You know how that goes! Sure, I do Morghan; just know the invitation stands if you need an escape. Thank you! I appreciate that, Tabitha. They bided each other goodbye as they parted ways, walking towards their vehicles.

Morghan's drive was a little longer than Tabitha's because she lived right outside of the Frisco, Dallas town line. She put her Tory Burkes sunglasses on and turned the music up to prepare for the mid-day traffic she'd have to endure to get across town; then she sped off into the sunlight. Thinking about the conversation she and Tabitha had about their losses at lunch made her think about Amiya Rain on the way home. Passing several children at play in the parks didn't make the drive any easier. Everything reminded Morghan of Amiya. Every child's voice or passing anything associated with children brought memory back to Morghan's harsh reality. She missed her daughter deeply, and no matter what she did, nothing would bring her back.

As she pulled into the driveway of her home, she removed her glasses and pulled down the overhead mirror to check her eyes. She had cried the whole way home and didn't want Brian to notice. Alright, Morghan, pull it together. Brian doesn't need to see you like this again. We don't need to have any more unsettling conversations. He's already skeptical about Tabitha's and my relationship; no need for him to think she's made me cry in the middle of the day. She took several deep breaths and made her way into the house.

"Hey babe, you're home! Brian met her at the door with the biggest kiss. I missed you!"

"Hey, babe Morghan replied in a low tone.

"How was your lunch date with Tabitha?"

"It was good, babe; I brought you back some appetizers. I know how much you love those wings and potato skins from Hurricanes."

"Oh, thanks, love! I was just gonna find myself a quick bite in the kitchen before I headed back upstairs to work. Nope, I was thinking of you, so you don't have to do that now. Morghan handed Brian the bag and walked toward their master bedroom.

"Wait bae, I want to talk to you about something."

"Ok, go ahead, I'm listening! How would you feel about us having a small barbecue this weekend? You know, how we used to before." Brian pauses to see Morghan's reaction before he finishes his sentence. Morghan looked up, surprised at the gesture.

"It's ok, Brian! I know we haven't hosted anything in a while."

"I'm ok with having a small gathering. Who will we invite?"

"Well, I was thinking the usual clan.

"Ok, that's cool; I could use some entertainment around here. I'll invite Tabitha too!"

"Um ok, do you think she'll fit in? You know how our friends can be with newcomers."

"I think she'll fit in great. I'm sure she could use a night of fun and laughs as well. It will be good for her to get to know some people in town. She hasn't been here that long and doesn't know anyone yet."

"Ok, but I'm blaming you if this doesn't go well." Brian snickered as he took his lunch and headed up the stairs.

"It will be fine babe, I promise."

"Ok, well when I'm done work in a few hours, we can go to the store to grab a few things."

"Ok, I'll make the invite calls to let everyone know."

Chapter Three
Tabitha

She was sitting in her black Range Rover with the windows tinted to the point where if you didn't know it was her, you couldn't see who it was. Tabitha agonized about entering her home alone yet again. Jerimmi Sr and Junior had been gone almost a year now, and it still bothered her to enter the house, knowing they wouldn't be there to greet her. Tabitha fought back tears as she sat in the vehicle listening to the love song playlist she and Jerrimi created before his demise. She stared at the home that was supposed to be a new beginning for their family. She remembered when she first arrived in Texas and their last call.

"The familiar sounds of Lafitte, Louisiana were faded away as Tabitha stood in the huge new home in Frisco Texas. Boxes were stacked against the walls, and the home smelled of fresh paint. Tabitha glanced at her phone to check who was calling her. She had been waiting to hear from her husband Jerrimi, who was still in Louisiana with their son Junior. She couldn't wait to share her excitement about how beautiful the house was.

"Hey, babe!" Jerrimi's voice crackled through the line. Warm and comforting despite the distance. Hi sweetheart!

How's everything going? Tabitha asked, leaning against the kitchen counter."

"We're almost packed up. Just finishing loading the last boxes on the truck, he replied. Junior has been a real trooper, though he keeps asking when we'll be there."

"Just tell him we're one sleep away! Tabitha laughed softly. This place is already starting to feel like home, but it's a bit lonely without you two. I can't believe you guys are finally on your way."

"Yeah, it will be nice to have everyone back together again."

"Just wait until you see it! The neighborhood is great, and I found a fantastic park nearby for Junior. He's going to love it." Tabitha's excitement bubbled over."

"Sounds perfect. I can't wait for the three of us to explore together. Any updates on the job? Jerrimi asked, his tone shifting to a more serious note."

"Just the usual orientation stuff. Everyone seems really nice, and I think I'm going to fit in well. It feels good to be starting this chapter of our lives finally. She said, her heart filled with hope about the future."

"That's good to hear. I know how much this means to you. I am a little worried about moving Junior, though. You know how he can be with change."

"I know, but we'll make it work. Kids are resilient. Plus, we'll be there to help him through it. Just remind him of all the adventures that await us in Texas! Tabitha encouraged."

"Speaking of adventures, do you think we'll have time to hit up that BBQ place you mentioned? I've been craving some good brisket," Jerrimi asked with a hint of humor in his voice.

"Absolutely! We'll make it our first outing. Just imagine the three of us digging into some Texas BBQ! I'm drooling already, just thinking about it." Tabitha chuckled.

As they spoke, Tabitha felt the distance between them begin to close, the excitement of their new life ahead washing over her. Just one more day, love. I can't wait to see you both.

"Same here. We'll be there by noon tomorrow. Just keep the coffee hot, okay?" Jerrimi replied, his voice filled with affection.

"Always. I'll be waiting for you both with open arms." Tabitha promised, her heart filled with anticipation.

"Alright, I better get back to it. We'll be together soon, and then the real adventure begins. And don't forget, we still need to talk about that thing I found."

"Right, I haven't forgot babe. I can't wait! Drive safe, okay? Love you both so much."

Love you too, Tabitha. See you tomorrow!" The call ended, leaving Tabitha smiling as she looked around her empty home.

Tomorrow would mark the beginning of a new life, and she couldn't wait to explore what it would be like."

The piercing wail of the siren sound of the ambulance that was riding by immediately shook Tabitha out of her daydream. She looked around to see if anyone was around before she got out of the car and ran up the steps to the front door.

Riiiiing, Riiiiing! Her phone began to ring as she took the key out of the door. She reached down into her purse to get it before it stopped.

"Hello!" She answered hastily.

"Hey Tabitha, this is Morghan. I know we spoke about hanging out later, but I need to stay back to go to the store this evening with Brian."

"Ok, Morghan, it's alright! We can do it another day."

"Well, actually, I wanted to see if you were up for a little shindig tomorrow evening. That's why we need to go to the grocery store tonight. Brian and I are having a little get-together. Just a few friends over for some food and laughs. I sure could use some of both. I'm hoping you will come."

"Umm, I won't know anyone there, and I don't want to be a third wheel. "

"Oh, don't worry Tabitha, you will get to know everyone. And you won't be a third, fourth, or fifth wheel. Please say you'll join us."

"Uhm, ok, I will be there!" Great! You'll finally get to meet Brian, too." I can't wait! Should I bring anything?

"Nope! Just yourself. Be here around 6:30. I'll text you the address. Alright, I'll see you tomorrow.

"Ok, bye." They both ended the call.

Tabitha sat her bags down and walked up the stairs towards her bedroom. She stopped halfway up the stairway and looked at the family portrait of her Jerrimi and Junior. She gently touched the photo with a slight smile on her face. "I really miss you guys, she whispered."

Chapter Four
Just Like Old Times

66 Aww, Bae, it really looks good in here. I thought you would have needed my help, but you seemed to have done your thing."

"Thanks, baby! Brian replies with a quick kiss. I do need you to taste this for me."

"What is it? Morghan asked as she hesitantly opened her mouth to taste." "My secret rib sauce that you love so much."

"Mmm, she savored the spoonful of warm barbecue sauce. That's delicious as usual."

"That's what I was hoping you'd say. I'm almost done with everything here. The Hord 'oeuvres are ready, and so are the salads and chicken. Once I sauce up these ribs, we will be ready."

"Ok, great! The guess should be here soon."

"Yup, Erich is in the neighborhood and Claudette and Cory are on the way. They had to wait for the babysitter to arrive."

"Ok, well, let me freshen up and get the grill smell off of me before they get here. I'll be right back!"

Ding Dong! The doorbell rings as Brian walks away to the bedroom.

"I'm sure that's Erich!" Morghan turns to answer the door." Hey E, she greets him at the door with a hug."

"Morghan, how are you?"

"I'm good today she responded. Come on in, make yourself at home as you normally do."

"You know I will! Where's my boy?"

"He's in the back getting changed. Knock on the door; he may be almost done." Erich heads straight to the bedroom to see Brian. Ding Dong, the doorbell rings again.

"I'll get it," Morghan turns back around to get the door. The guest begins to arrive one by one. Before long, the house is filled with old friends and some family. Lastly, the doorbell rang with one guest who had not gotten there yet. Morghan opened the door, expecting it to be Tabitha.

"Hey, lady!" Tabitha greets Morghan.

"Well, heyyy Tabitha, you look stunning!" Morghan admires Tabitha standing there wearing an all-black maxi dress with flat silver sandals. Her hair was bone straight about midway down her back.

"Wow, look at the hair! I didn't realize how long it was because of the up bun you always wear. Come in, girl, meet the gang." Morghan grabs Tabitha's hand and pulls her into the house. She guides her to the kitchen area, where most of the guests are. "Hey everyone, I would like you to meet my new friend Tabitha."

"Hey, Tabitha," everyone yells.

"Tabitha, this is my husband, Brian."

"Nice to finally meet you Brian; Morghan talks about you always.

"Nice to meet you too Tabitha. It's good to put a face to the person my wife spends so much time with." Brian smiles as he shakes Tabitha's hand.

"Oh, cut it out" Morghan softly punches Brian on the arm. Ignore him, Tabitha! And this is my best friend/sister Claudette. Claudette this is Tabitha, my friend I told you about from the grief meetings."

"Nice to meet you, Claudette!"

"Same here Tabitha."

"This is her husband, Corey."

"Nice to meet you," Corey waves.

"And this fella who can't stop eating up all the food is Erich. Erich this is Tabitha!" Erich turns to acknowledge Tabitha as he's making a plate of food. His eyes spoke before he could utter a word.

"Hey Tabitha," he said slowly while gazing at her up and down. "You are beautiful!"

"Leave my friend alone please E!" Morghan pulled Tabitha away before she could respond. "Are you hungry she asked?"

"No, but I would like a bottle of water."

"Sure, help yourself! I would eat something before it's gone. That Erich character has a never-ending pit at the bottom of his stomach." They both laugh!

"I'll be sure to get something before it's gone."

"Ok, let's go out back," she invited Tabitha, leaving the other guest inside.

"I love this house, Morghan." Tabitha admired Morghan and Brian's home. "This is really beautiful."

"Thanks, girl! I just lit the firepit so we can sit out here."

"Ok, good!

"I'm glad you were able to make it Tabitha; I know you were kind of hesitant on the phone yesterday."

"Yeah, I was a little nervous about it, but I figured I could use an outing. I haven't been out anywhere in a long time. Thanks for inviting me!"

"Sure thing, girl! It was all Brian's idea. We used to do this often before; Morghan was hesitant to finish her sentence."

"I understand Morghan."

"Yeah, he thought it would be good for the both of us."

"Things like this are always nice. Having friends and family around is a good way to help with healing."

"Tabitha, do you have family here with you in Texas?" I don't think I ever asked you that."

"No, everyone is in Louisiana. I do need to make a trip there soon, though, to see everyone. I'm sure that would be nice!" Tabitha replied!

"Hey ladies, y'all just left us in there," Claudette yells from the door as she approaches the firepit to join Morghan and Tabitha.

"Come on out Claudette, Morghan invites. Join us!

"We were just talking about Tabitha visiting her family in Louisiana soon."

"Oh, that's where you're from?" Claudette asked.

"Yes, born and raised!"

"I can hear the accent now, Claudette acknowledges. How did you end up here in Texas? If I may ask!"

"It's a long story, but I moved here for work."

"Oh, what do you do?"

"I'm a financial analyst for a pretty big company here in Texas."

"Oh, Morghan, she does something similar to you."

"Yeah, I told her I could probably use her expertise sometimes."

"For what? Moghan, you own the company!" Tabitha's eyes widened in disbelief.

"You what?" You told me you were in finances not that you own a whole finance company. "She does. Claudette speaks confidently. My best friend is a whole boss!"

"Claudette, Morghan interferes. Don't do that!"

"Do what, she asked. Well, you are!"

"Yeah, but we don't need to advertise that. I like to say I'm in finances." "She's so modest," Claudette looks at Tabitha.

"That's great Morghan; you don't need to be ashamed of that," Tabitha replies; that's a great accomplishment.

"I'm not ashamed; I just don't broadcast it. I never want to lead with that. I like my friendships to be genuine, you know. I do own a small financial company here in Texas."

"Ok, I get it," Tabitha responds.

"So how long," Claudette is interrupted before she could finish her sentence as Brian, Eric, and Cory walk out to join them around the fire pit.

"Hey wife, Corey calls out to Claudette. I was wondering where you disappeared to."

"I'm here husband, just chatting with the ladies." They all sit next to the ladies.

"So Tabitha, Erich calls out. Are you from around here?"

"I'm not from far."

"Good, so that means you won't be hard to find."

"I didn't know anyone was looking for me," Tabitha replied.

They all laugh cohesively.

"Well, you know now!" Erich gazes into Tabitha's eyes.

"Umm, excuse me, everyone, on that note, I'm gonna go see if there's any food left."

"I can help you," Erich offers.

"No, I think I can handle it, but thank you!"

Tabitha goes into the house and makes her way around the table, picking up anything that was meatless or had seafood in it.

"Yuck she whispers as she passes the tray of ribs and grilled chicken. Flesh is so disgusting," she thought as she bypassed them. Leaving the table with only some devilled eggs and a spoonful of seafood salad, she made her way through the huddle of people who were standing around talking.

"This house is really beautiful." Tabitha admired the spiral staircase with the clear banister that led into the shiny white and gray marble flooring that screamed riches. "Wow, she really is a boss. Aww, this must be little Amiya." Tabitha paused at the wall of photos of Morghan, Brian, and Amiya near the staircase. She paid close attention to one photo in particular. It was of Brian and Morghan in a complete black and white shot. The realistic look of the photo quickly caught

Tabitha's eye. Something about Brians eyes in the photo spoke to Tabitha.

"They're a beautiful couple, aren't they?" A women stood next to Tabitha and spoke.

"Yes, they are! So is this photo!" They both stared in silence as if they were in an art museum.

"Tabitha, a voice yelled! Did you get some food?"

"Yes, I did, Brian, thank you!"

"Good, Morghan wanted me to check on you."

"I appreciate it." Tabitha tried to avoid eye contact with Brian, but she found it a bit hard to do. His beautiful hazel eyes were just as stunning as they were in the photo. His dark brown skin color reminded her of Jerrimi Sr. "May I use your restroom?"

"Sure, it's right around the corner here. Brian directed Tabitha. Here, let me take that for you; I'll get rid of it for you."

"Thanks, Brian."

"Not a problem." Tabitha makes her way to the bathroom.

"Hey Brian, Claudette calls out just as Brian turns to throw out Tabitha's plate.

"What's up Claudy!"

"Nothing, how is my girl really doing?" Claudette asked with concern.

"She's hanging in there. She's been better since attending the grief meetings. I've actually been seeing her smile a lot more."

"So you think the meetings are helping?"

"I think so, and she's been talking to Tabitha since meeting her there, so I think it's helping."

"Tabitha, what's her deal?"

"What do you mean?"

"Well, she has been spending a lot of time with her, it seems; what do you think about her?"

"Well, I'm just meeting her for the first time tonight with you all, but she seems solid. Did she lose someone, or does she work there?"

"No, I don't work there Claudette! Remember I told you I work for a finance company? Tabitha interjects as she returns from the bathroom and overhears the conversation."

"Oh, that's right! I'm sorry, I must have forgot."

"I actually did lose someone, two someone's to be exact. My husband and my son! Claudette and Brian look at each other in disbelief.

"Excuse me, I'm going to head back outside to find Morghan." Tabitha squeezes through Brian and Claudette, heading towards the patio door.

"Morghan, thank you for everything; I'm getting ready to head out.

"Tabitha, are you ok?"

"Yes, I'm fine, everything was good!"

"Ok, Morghan replies. You sure you don't want to stay longer?"

"I'm sure, love, I need to get some rest. I have some stuff to do tomorrow." "Alright then!"

"Hey Tabitha, I can walk you to your car," Erich stands to walk Tabitha out.

"Erich, thank you, but I'm good! My car is right out front; I'll be fine." She says as she reaches down to hug Morghan.

"Call me tomorrow sometime, and we can talk."

"Ok, well, at least text me to let me know you made it home."

"Ok, I will!" Tabitha waves goodbye and heads to her car.

A few more hours passed and everyone else said their goodbyes.

"Thanks, Claudette and Cory, for helping with the clean-up."

"You know it's no problem, guys!" Cory replied. Well we better get home to the rug rats.

"Yea, were gonna go get the kiddos. I love y'all, and we'll see you soon. Call me sister. Claudette kisses Morghan on the cheek. See you soon," she hugs Brian. They both see them at the door and out of their car.

"Bye, guys," they both wave as the car backs out of the driveway. Brian grabs Morghan hand and leads her back into the house.

"That was nice, babe!"

"It really was! I'm glad everyone was able to make it."

"Yeah, me too! It was a reminder of old times. I love you Brian; thank you for doing this for me." You're so welcome bae; I just wanted to see you smile again. It's been tuff for us both, and we needed a release. I'll start the dishwasher and finish up the kitchen. No, you've done enough tonight love. Leave it; I'll get it in the morning. Morghan kisses Brian softly on the lips. She blows out the candles on the counter and takes Brian's hand, leading him to the bedroom. They enter the room, closing the door behind them. **For a moment, they just stood there, holding each other in the quiet of their bedroom.**

The weight of the day slipped away in the comfort of his embrace, and Morgan felt the familiar steadiness that only Brian could provide. You look tired," he said softly, brushing a strand of hair from her cheek. His fingers lingered there, tracing the curve of her jaw. "It's a good kind of tired," she whispered, her gaze meeting his. "The kind that makes me want to end the night like this." Brian leaned down, pressing his forehead to hers. "Like this?" he whispered before brushing his lips against hers. The kiss started slow, a gentle exploration that quickly deepened as Brian tilted her head slightly, his other hand resting on her lower back. Morghan slowly began to remove her blouse, unbuttoning one at a time. She pulls

Brian t shirt over his head and drops it to the floor. They kiss again passionately as Brian begins to remove Morghan's bra.

"I think we should take a shower," she whispers as she nibbles on his left ear. She leads him into the bathroom, where they remove the rest of their clothing. Brian enters the steaming shower first and welcomes Morghan in to join him.

"The temperature is just the way you like it" he warns. He embraces her waist close to him as they take a moment to enjoy the hot flowing water. Brian then sits down on the shower bench. He guides Morghan to him and straddles her across his thighs. Morghan slowly places herself directly over his rock-hard penis. She slowly slides down on him, enjoying the feeling as her vaginal walls grasp onto his hardness. They both release a moan that ensures they have missed each other's touch. After minutes of friction, they both release a sigh of relief. Morghan falls motionless into Brians chest as they both pause with satisfaction. They kiss once more as Morghan removes herself from Brian and they both proceed with their showers. Morghan leaves Brian behind once she's done. She dries off and, grabs her white night shirt out of the drawer and pulls the covers back and climbs into the bed. Brian follows shortly after to find Morghan already asleep.

"I love you babe; he pulls the cover over her and gently kisses her on the forehead. Goodnight!"

Chapter Five
Tabitha

As Tabitha pulled into her driveway, the glow of the streetlight glared down on her vehicle. She turned off the car and sat there in complete silence. Her thoughts rambled away in many directions, some with exhaustion from the day of events that took place and some with a little frustration about what took place at the barbecue. She slowly began to make her way out of the car and into the house. She tossed her keys onto the counter and began removing her clothing as she walked up the steps, heading straight to the bathroom. Urh, I can't take this smell any longer, she complained as the aroma of grilled meats and smokey spices lingered on her everywhere. Leaving a trail of clothing from the bottom of the steps to the shower, she turned on the water and immediately got in. Standing directly under the showerhead, Tabitha allowed the water to hit her face as she stood there holding her head back welcoming the steady flow. Flashes of memories began to rush through her mind.

"I've been waiting for you all day!"

"I'm here now!"

Tabitha responded with a gentle kiss. She embraced the strong hands that caressed her body.

"I've missed you so much," Tabitha whispered.

She closed her eyes and reached out to grab the body that was attached to the voice. She suddenly realized there was nobody. Just the memories of Jerrimi Sr and what used to be.

Tabitha finished her shower and turned off the faucet. She reached for her towel and stepped out of the shower to dry off. Not bothering to apply lotion or dress for bed, Tabitha put on her black robe and hurried to her bedroom. She smothered her face into her pillow and cried until she fell off to sleep.

The Next Morning

Buzzzzz! The sound of the alarm awakens Tabitha. She reaches without opening her eyes to shut off the jarring sound. Buzzzzz! The alarm sounds again 5 minutes later. Alright already! I'm awake! Tabitha shuts off the alarm a second time and then reaches for her cell phone. Why is it 6 am already? She whispered. She took a deep breath and began to move her body up in the bed. Shoot! It's Saturday, I forgot to change the stupid alarm, she thought to herself. With nothing planned for the day, Tabitha laid in bed for a few more minutes. No, I might as well start my day since I'm already awake. She sat up on the side of the bed and began to move her body, stretching from side to side before she stood up. She pulled back the curtains to allow the sunlight to enter the dark room and began to make up her bed. She then made her way to the bathroom to brush her teeth and wash her face. On her way down to the kitchen, she retrieved the clothing she had left on the stairwell the night before, taking them to the laundry room. She turned on the television to drown out all of the Saturday quietness that filled her home as she passed by the family room. Turning on Juniors favorite Saturday cartoon show, she smiles at his photo on the counter. As she makes her usual cup of lavender tea, Tabitha goes out on the deck to sit.

The air was crisp with the lingering chill of the early morning end-of-summer weather. The smell of the morning dew reminded her of early mornings back home in Louisiana when she would pick apples from her grandmother's apple tree on Saturdays before breakfast. With her favorite mug cradled between her fingers as the steam danced upward, carrying the calming scent of lavender and fresh lemon, Tabitha listened closely to the birds chirping as it was a morning symphony of life. She took a slow sip of her tea, savoring the moment. She let her gaze drift off into her garden, where she grew fruits and vegetables in remembrance of her mom-mom Earnestine. It gave her so much joy to listen to the mix of high-pitched notes that filled the morning air. The sounds invited a peaceful ambiance that she needed to help the day get started. As she sank deeper into her thoughts, her mind wandered back to a distant moment in her life when things were not so peaceful.

Morris Jeff Community High School

The year was 2004. Tabitha had spent her whole four years of high school being a loner. Outside of her timid, quiet, introverted nature, her thin, awkward body frame with acne and bifocal glasses made it even harder for her to make friends in school. Tabitha spent most school days walking the halls and eating lunch alone. The mysterious rumor that spread around the school like wildfire about her grandmother being a queen of voodoo and black magic did not sit well with her classmates. Tabitha endured the funny stares and the rude whispering that went on as she passed the students in the halls. That was until one day, sitting in history class. Tabitha walked into class with her book bag on her right shoulder unaware of the bag being open. As she turned to sit at her usual desk in that class, several of her books fell onto the floor. She bent over to pick them up as everyone stared.

"Let me help you," one voice came over and spoke.

"No, I have it" she said without making eye contact with the voice.

"Here you go," the voice spoke again, and Tabitha looked up and met his eyes. It was the famous school football quarterback Raymond Lee. Tabitha never paid any attention to any of the boys in school especially none that were on the football team. Her confidence was too low to ever think that anyone, let alone a school Joc would ever look her way.

"Thank you," she uttered as she hurried and grabbed the book away from Raymond. She quickly put the books on her desk and sat in her seat, never to look his way again. Her heart pounded as she had never been that close to anyone before.

"What's your name?" Raymond asked as he sat down next to her.

"Tabitha" she responded without looking at him again.

"Hi Tabitha, I'm Raymond! Nice to meet you!"

He held out his hand for Tabitha to shake it, but she never reached her hand out.

"Why don't you ever talk to anyone, Tabitha?"

"Talk to anyone about what?" Tabitha responded, confused.

"Anything! I just always see myself alone, not talking to anybody.

"Don't you have any friends?"

Tabitha takes a deep breath and shrugs her shoulder.

"Why do you care if I have friends or not?"

"I'm just saying, it has to be real lonely walking around all day not talking to anyone. I mean, we are here for like 7 hours or something like that."

"Unless you're watching me the whole day, how would you know if I talk to anyone or not?"

"I guess you're right! But I still never see you talking!"

"I'm talking now, aren't I?"

Raymond smirks and shakes his head.

"I guess you're right!"

Raymond turns to face the teacher as she begins to talk, interrupting their conversation.

After class, Tabitha packs up her books and hurry's out of the class, trying to avoid any more talking with Raymond Lee. She makes a right turn out of the classroom to find him waiting there for her.

"Hey, Tabitha!" He calls out to her and starts walking alongside her.

"Hey Raymond, what is it?"

"You can call me Ray."

"No, I'd rather Raymond!"

"Everyone calls me Ray!"

I'm not everyone, Raymond."

"What is it you want?"

"I don't want anything! I just figured I'd walk you to your next class."

"That's ok, I know the way! Thanks anyway, Raymond!"

Tabitha rushes along, walking ahead of Raymond. She loses him in the crowd of students before he can respond.

Later that evening, while Tabitha is getting ready to do homework, she reaches into the front pocket of her book bag for a pen. Suddenly she feels a piece of paper that she does not recall putting there. Tabitha pulls the balled-up piece of notebook paper out of her bag and opens it. It reads!

"Call me 504 231 0126 Ray!!!"

Tabitha reads the paper over and over again in disbelief.

"How did he, was her first thought." She suddenly feels a queasy rush to her stomach. She drops the paper and runs to the bathroom to vomit.

"Are you ok Tabitha?" Her mother calls out.

Tabitha wipes her mouth with her arm and yells out to her mother.

"Yes, I'm fine! My stomach is just a little upset mother?"

Tabitha washed her hands and goes back to her room, where she dropped the paper with Raymond Lee's phone number.

"This can't be true! She thinks to herself.

"Why would he want me to call him? Raymond Lee has never once looked my way, and now he wants me to call him." This has to be a practical joke! And I refuse to be the butt of it!" Tabitha balls the piece of paper back up and throws it in the trash. She resumes her homework assignment as planned.

About an hour passed and Tabitha could not shake the butterflies that had made a home in her belly since finding Raymond's number in her bag. She closed her last assignment and grabbed the piece of paper out of the trashcan. She unbaled it once again and stared at the number in disbelief.

Never planning to call the number, Tabitha toys with the thought of her and Raymond becoming a thing. She imagined waiting for him after a game where he gave her a big hug after a win and placed his team jacket around her arms to let everyone know she was his. Tabitha smiled at the possibility.

"He is handsome! She thought. He's tall and has a great-looking body. What could he possibly want with me?"

Tabitha stood in the mirror, starring at her awkward, thin body. She turned side to side, trying to imagine what she'd look like if she had a better shape. She removed her glasses and let her long black hair, which she always wore in a bun, down. Does he really like me? Or is this a stupid prank that he wants to play on me, she thought. If this was a game, how could she make Raymond really attractive to her was all she could think about in that moment.

Tabitha put the piece of paper in her pocket and left out of her bedroom. She went down the hall to her grandmother's room. Knock Knock! She softly knocked on the door.

"Mom-Mom, are you asleep?"

"No baby, come on in!" Grandmom replied.

Tabitha gently opens the door and slowly walks in.

"Hey Mom-mom"

"Hi, you doing Tab"

"Umm, I'm fine! I just wanted to check in on you mom-mom."

Tabitha looked around the room filled with the scent of peppermint and lavender. She observed all of the dolls, crystals, and mirrors that filled the corners of Grandma Earnestine's room. She always noticed the black and white photos on the walls of a younger Earnestine and Tabitha's mother when she was a young girl. Tabitha was always drawn to her grandmother's world of whispers of magic and the supernatural. She took a deep breath as she stepped further inside to find Grandma Earnestine sitting in her rocking chair. Tabitha walked over to her and bent over to kiss her on the cheek. She couldn't help but notice the trinkets on the dresser, each one carrying a story and a secret.

"Grandma, I wanted to talk to you about something important."

Earnestine sat forward in her seat, her long silver and black hair cascading down her shoulders in loose waves, her deep brown eyes widened with curiosity.

"What's on your mind, sweety?" She motioned for Tabitha to sit on the edge of the bed across from her.

Tabitha was hesitant to move forward, not knowing how her grandmother would respond.

"It's about a boy!" She reaches into her pocket and retrieves the wrinkled-up piece of paper. He gave me this today! He had never noticed me before, but all of a sudden today he did. I don't know what to do. He's a star football player, mom-mom. Why does he all of a sudden want me to call him? I thought maybe you could help and tell me what to do."

Grandmom Earnestine's expression shifted, showing a deepening understanding.

"I see! She replied as she reached out for the paper. Do you like him?"

"I mean, he is cute, I never thought about if I liked him."

"Well baby, before I can help, I would need to know a few things, and that is one of them. You know love is a powerful force, so we need to approach it with care."

"Love? Mom-mom, who said anything about love?"

Grandmom Earnestine leaned back in her rocking chair, tapping her fingers on her left knee.

"Tab, I don't suggest using magic as a tool for manipulation. I use it as a guide, an influence but I try very hard not to use it to control another's heart against their will. Now, because he gave you this number, I will assume he already likes you. If you don't like him, then there's no point in trying to control this situation. I would just let him be!"

"I do like him! Tabitha quickly responded. But I didn't say anything about using magic!"

Her grandmother smiled gently with a knowing in her eyes.

"Ok, then! There are some ways to attract someone's attention without bending their will. Your intentions matter! If you truly like him, you want him to genuinely like you in return for who you are, not because of a spell."

"What do you mean? Tabitha asked, her curiosity piqued."

"Let's think of it this way, grandmom Earnestine replied, rising up from her chair to her feet and walking slowly over to her dresser. She picked up a small vial filled with a gold shimmering liquid.

"This is a charm for attraction- not to manipulate but to enhance your natural allure. It can boost your confidence and help you express yourself more openly."

Tabitha's eyes widened as her mom-mom handed her the vial.

"How does it work?"

"Before you see him, take a few drops and say this incantation." Grandmom Earnestine instructed. Her voice softened as she recited the words that had been passed down through generations.

"Remember Tab, the charm will work best when you believe in yourself."

Tabitha nodded with excitement and nervousness swirling inside her.

"I'll do it, mom-mom! I promise to be myself, and if he really likes me, this will help us."

Tabitha took the vial and kissed her grandmother on the cheek once more before leaving the room.

Tabitha returned to her bedroom and glanced at the number once more. Feeling empowered by her grandmother, she picked up the phone and dialed the number.

"Hello!" A deep voice answered on the first ring.

"Hel, hello, Tabitha stuttered. May I speak to Raymond?"

"Speaking! He replied.

"It's Tabitha from school."

"I knew that was you!"

From that moment on Tabitha and Raymond Lee became a thing. Just as her Grandmom had advised her, she used the vial every day before she would see Raymond. They hung out during and after school for weeks. Tabitha attended football games she had never once thought to attend before. She had become unrecognizable to everyone, including herself. Things were going so well within Tabitha's newfound relationship and life.

One day in between classes, Tabitha went into the girl's restroom to use the bathroom. While finishing up in the stall, she overheard a familiar voice come in with two other individuals. They were cheerleaders, and the familiar voice was of Raymond ex-girlfriend, Chastity Reynolds. Chastity had not been happy with Raymond's new relationship, and she made it known every chance she got. Tabitha didn't want to deal with her and her obnoxious squad of peons, so she stood on top of the toilet seat so they wouldn't know anyone was in there.

"Chastity, did you see your boo with his new hamster girlfriend?"

"Girl please! Do you think I'm even a bit worried about Ray and his pity project?" He doesn't like that girl any more than she likes herself. He just needed something to do while I had him on punishment. That's all it is."

The girls all laugh while fixing their hair and makeup in the mirror.

"But since it's getting close to prom, I think I may go ahead and take him off punishment. We do need to get our outfits together. And I do miss him! I think he's suffered enough by now. I'll have him remove my placeholder today, as a matter of fact."

The girls all look at Chastity with approval as they all walk out of the restroom together.

Tabitha fights back tears as she waits for them to leave. She slowly climbs down off the toilet and walks out shortly after them.

Back to Life

The clinking of her mug against the table brought Tabitha back to the present. She blinked to shake off the nostalgia that was beginning to become heavy on her mind. The sun had risen higher, warming her face. It was time to face her day. Just as she stood up, her phone buzzed on the table, startling her. Glancing down at the screen, she saw a message from Morghan.

"Good morning, friend! Hope I'm not waking you. Are you free for lunch today?" With a quick response, Tabitha agreed to meet at their favorite spot in town. She gathered her blanket and mug and headed inside to prepare for the day's date.

Chapter Six
The Morning After

The morning sun streamed through a crack in the curtains, streaming a ray of light across the bedroom. Morghan had been awake for some time listening to Brian snore and playing games on her phone. She hadn't woken up this early in months. As she pulled herself up from the cozy sheets, she glanced over at Brian, who had not moved an inch. She smiled at him, remembering their night together. Morghan slipped out of the room and into the kitchen, trying not to awaken Brian. She opened the blinds and turned on the coffee maker to make some for her and Brian. She looked around the kitchen, her mind wandering back to the barbecue. As she poured her first cup of coffee, she thought back to Tabitha and Erich. Just then, she heard the door creak shut. Brian emerged from the bedroom, rubbing his eyes and yawning.

"Good morning, sleepy head." Morghan teased, handing him a cup of coffee.

"Morning, babe! Is it too early for a recap of last night?"

"Not at all! I was just thinking about Erich and Tabitha. Did you notice how he kept trying to get her attention? I mean, he was relentless in trying to walk her to her car before she left."

Brian laughed, recalling the moment. "Yeah, I saw how she shot him down each time he tried. I think he really likes her."

Morghan agreed, her mind racing with possibilities. "I wonder if she's ready to date."

"I don't know Morghan. She seemed a little upset when she overheard us talking about her, and she mentioned she had loss her husband and son."

"Wait, what? Who were you talking about her with?"

"Well I showed her to the bathroom, then Claudette asked me what I knew about her. I told her I was just meeting her as she was. The next thing I know, Tabitha appeared after she heard Claudette asked if she worked at the grief center or if she had lost someone."

"Are you kidding me? I told you she had loss her son!"

"Yes, but you never said her husband too!"

Morghan shakes her head in disbelief.

"How did she lose her husband and son, Morghan?"

"They were in a car accident on the way moving here. Tabitha came ahead, and they were coming with the rest of the things and never made it."

"Oh no! Babe, I'm so sorry! Brian pulls Morghan close to him to embrace her. I didn't know, and when Claudette asked, I didn't get a chance to answer because she came out."

"That explains her rushing out of here to leave."

I hope she's not upset with us."

"Well, I texted her this morning to see if she wanted to meet for lunch."

"You text her already? Morghan, we just woke up! Why is she the first thing on your mind?"

"Brian don't start! I just figured you would be busy today. Remember you have that meeting this afternoon. So I just thought I'd go hang with her for a few hours until you were done."

"Yea, I remember!" Brian lowers his head somberly.

"What do you think about us inviting them over for a night of Pizza and board games?

"Morghan, you just said she lost her husband. Now you want to play matchmaker?"

"Well, I don't think it will hurt to get to know someone whether they become a thing or decide just to be friends; she could use a new face to talk to from time to time. She only has me here right now." Who knows what can happen?" Brian shakes his head in disagreement but agrees to go forth with Morghan's plan.

"When do you want to do this Morghan? They just met last night; I think tonight will be too soon."

"I'll talk to her this afternoon and see what she says. I think next weekend would be good, though."

"I think you're getting ahead of yourself. Let's not push this too hard. They need to figure it out naturally."

"That's true Brian, Morghan conceded. But it can't hurt to give them a little nudge in the right direction."

They sat together a while longer sipping their coffee and chatting about the night before. Morghan couldn't shake the feeling that Tabitha was upset about what had happened with Claudette. She didn't mention it again to Brian, but she was eager to get to the restaurant to see how she was.

Chapter Seven
Day Date

The charming little café on the corner of 5th and Main was already filled when Tabitha arrived. She had beaten Morghan there, so she went in to grab a seat before they were all gone. Tabitha picked a booth close to the window facing the front door of the restaurant where she could see Morghan when she arrived. She also enjoyed watching the people out the window, on the horse and carriage rides up and down Mainstreet, which was an every Saturday event. The crowds would pour in to shop the little boutiques and marketplaces that were up and down the sidewalks.

Tabitha scanned the menu for her usual items but waited to order them.

"I'll just have water with lemon for now." She told the waiter, who was a cheerful young man with a friendly smile. Tabitha glanced around the café. Couples chatted intimately, and families gathered around tables filled with fresh bakery bread and butter while they waited for their orders to arrive. The sound of laughter mingled with the clinking of glasses. She couldn't help but smile at the lively atmosphere feeling a wave of contentment wash over her as she thought about Jerrimi and how they would have dates and people watched as they would wait for food and drinks.

A few minutes passed, and as she was beginning to lose herself in thought, the door swung open and in walked Morghan. Removing her sunglasses from her face to the top of her head, Morghan scanned the room, looking for Tabitha. When their eyes met, Morghan waved and called out as she made her way over to the booth.

"Hey Lady! Sorry, I'm late! You know how that early Saturday traffic can be."

"No worries! I haven't been here that long," Tabitha replied, standing up to give her friend a warm hug. "You look great!"

Morghan smiled, sweeping her hair behind her left ear. "Thanks! You too! I love that top."

They both slid into the booth and began looking at the menu. "I already know what I want, but I didn't want to order without you. What are you getting?"

Morghan ran her eyes around the menu, checking her options; her lips tightened with concentration. "I think I'll have the avocado toast. I need something light after last night's barbecue."

Morghan's face lit up as she began to recount the night. "How did you like the gathering?" She leaned in asking Tabitha with her curiosity piqued.

"It was interesting, I thought. I enjoyed it for the most part."

"How did you like the food?"

"I didn't eat very much; I kind of picked over all the meat and went straight to the seafood and appetizers. But everything I had was delicious."

"That's right, I forgot you no longer eat meat."

I'm sorry; next time, I'll have Brian make some vegetarian options for you to enjoy. He's a pretty good cook."

"Don't worry about it, Morghan. No need to do anything special for me. I always figure it out according to what's available. This no-meat thing is new to me, so I'm just learning what I like and what I don't like as I go."

"Why did you decide to stop eating meat?"

"I just lost my appetite for it after Jerrimi left. Some of our favorite places were barbecue and steak restaurants. Once I could no longer enjoy them with him, I just could not stomach them anymore."

"Wow, Tabitha, that's a beautiful gesture." Morghan replied as she touched Tabitha's hand to show her empathy.

"Well, while we're on the subject of last night, let me apologize for Claudette's behavior. Brian told me about what took place when you came out of the bathroom."

"No need to apologize Morghan, Claudette is an adult, and she is free to do whatever she likes. I do sense a bit of a protection claim over you from her."

"Yeah, I can agree with that! Claudette and I have been friends since we were in grade school. She is the big sister I never had. So, in saying that, I will admit that she is a little overprotective of me."

"I get it! No harm done!"

"Ok, so moving on! Brian and I thought it would be a good idea to have a game night next weekend. Just you and I, him and Erich!" Morghan quickly turned her eyes back to the menu before Tabitha could respond.

"Uh, that sounds a bit like a double date Morghan! Homestyle addition! I think I will pass on that! I am not ready to be anyone's date! Especially not homeboys!" It's too soon for me even to entertain that!"

"Ok, I understand! I figured it was too soon, so that's why I wanted to do it as a gesture for Brian to get to know you. He complains that I spend too much time with you and so I just would like him to know you more. We saw how Erich seemed to be intrigued by you, so we thought inviting him would make it easier."

"Easier for who?" I'd rather not have him drooling over me all night! It was slightly uncomfortable, and he looked pitiful doing it." Tabitha replied, seeming a bit perturbed at the gesture of a double date.

"Ok, Tabitha, no worries, it was just a thought. If you are uncomfortable with it, then we don't have to do it."

The waiter returned before Tabitha could respond. "Are you ladies ready to order?"

"Yes, I'll take the quiche!" Tabitha replied first.

"And I'll have the avocado toast with a side of smoked salmon."

The waiter gathered their menus and returned to the kitchen to put their orders in.

Tabitha took a few deep breaths, her fingers tracing the rim of her glass. She felt bad for the way she had just reacted to Morghan's gesture.

"Listen Morghan; I didn't mean to offend you! It's just that I'm still wrestling with my feelings, trying to balance this new life that I've been thrown into. I miss my husband and my son so much! I don't know how to move forward without them. I know I have to…. I just don't want to force anything too soon. Morghan reaches across the table, placing her hand over Tabitha's.

"Tabitha, I get it; trust me, I do! Until the meetings, I had barely stepped foot out of bed for months. Brian helped me to get it together. It took a lot of time and effort from my husband to push me to start moving forward. It's the only thing I can do. Amiya is not coming back, and as much as I would give everything to have her here with her dad and me, it'll never be. So, although I don't know the pain of losing a husband, I do know the same pain of losing a child. It's a void that will never be refilled. I don't think you should force anything, either, but I do think moving forward is the only way to keep their memory alive. Or else we die along with them. I don't think that's what God intended. You deserve to have fun and enjoy life again. It's ok to enjoy yourself. I never knew Jerrimi, but if I had to guess, I know he would want you to move forth with life."

Tears peaked at the corner of Tabitha's eyes, but she blinked them away, feeling grateful for Morghan's support.

"You're right! I just need to take baby steps. I'll come over for game night next weekend."

"Okay, and if it feels too heavy when the time comes, we can always change plans. No pressure, I promise."

The waiter returns with their food, and they dig in, enjoying and savoring every bite.

Chapter Eight
Let the Games Begin

The week seemed to fly by quickly. Brian and Morghan were waist-deep in deadlines and pretty much had worked the week away. Morghan had to fly out of town for her first business meeting since Amiya's funeral. Brian finished his last security deadline just in time to pick her up from the airport. As he completed his call, he rushed off to get through the Friday traffic jams by the time Morghan plane landed.

As she stepped off the plane, Morghan adjusted the strap on her bag and blended in with the bustling of the other travelers making their way through Dallas Fort Worth International Airport. She was eager to see Brian, although she had only been gone two days. Her mind scrambled thinking about the task she had to get done before the game night later that evening.

She had not heard from Tabitha since their last lunch date a week ago, so she wasn't even shore if she stilled planned to attend. As she stepped out to the curbside, looking for Brian's Navy-Blue Mercedes Crossover, she pulled her phone out to send a quick text to Tabitha. "Hey Friend, long time no hear! Just checking to see if we're still on for tonight." Brian pulled up just as she finished her text. He jumped out to help her with her bags.

"My baby is back!" He called out as he approached her with his arms wide open to embrace her.

"Hey baby!" Morghan replied with a smile and a kiss on the lips. Brian reached for her luggage and headed to the trunk of the car.

"Thanks, love!"

"You know you don't lift any bags when I'm around."

"I know, right!" Morghan waited patiently for Brian to open her door.

"How was your trip?"

"It was surprisingly good, to be honest." Morghan replied as she fastened her seatbelt. "We were able to finalize everything for the new client, so we should receive the funds for that contract pretty soon."

"Cha Ching! I knew I could depend on you to run me my money. Brian teased with a joking smirk on his face.

"Whatever, babe! How about we go spend your money that I know posted today because I got the deposit notification this morning. We need to get a few things for the game night tonight."

"Yes, I figured that! Do you even know if Tabitha is coming?"

"I just texted her a few minutes ago, but she hasn't responded yet. I'm sure she'll be there."

"You mean you hope!"

"Well, I don't think anything has changed since we last talked. But you're right, I hope. Nonetheless, we still need to go shopping for you! Morghan reiterates, rubbing Brian on the shoulder with a devious smile.

The shopping spree was successful as far as Morghan was concerned. She picked up everything they needed for the game night, plus a few extra items at Brian's expense. Morgan grabbed her purse and unlocked the door, leaving Brian to handle the bags from the car. She stepped out of her shoes at the door and set her purse on the kitchen counter.

"I still haven't heard back from Tabitha," she thought to herself as she glanced at her watch to check to time. "We still have a few hours, so maybe by the time I wash the residual airport smell off of me, she'll call. Or text back." Morghan went to the bedroom to take a shower while Brian unpacked the bags and began to prepare for the night's festivities.

By the time she returned, the family room was filled with a slew of games and snacks. The sun had begun to set and beam through the large bay windows, leaving a bright shadow of natural light. Brian had spent the last 2 hours getting everything ready for their two guests. With the counter full of carefully curated snacks and drinks along with a charcuterie board of fruit and dips, Brian had just enough time to change clothes before the night began.

"Still nothing from ya girl yet?" He asked as he walked toward the bedroom.

Moghan had not checked her phone since getting out of the shower.

'I don't know, let's see!" She replied as she picked up her phone and began to scroll through the text messages.

"On the way!" was a short message from Tabitha.

"Great! She's on the way."

"Ok, well, let the games begin! Brian replied as he rushed off to change clothes. I'll be right back!

As the clock ticked closer to seven, Morghan fluffed the pillows on the sofa, her anxiety tinged with a hint of excitement. "I hope this goes well!" she told Brian.

"I'm not hoping for anything! This is just a game night for me. You are the one with the shenanigans going on. I told you we are not matchmakers."

"Just tell your boy to behave, and everything will be fine."

The doorbell rings, and Morghan and Brian pause and look at one another, surprised.

"I wonder which one is here first!" Brian sounded intrigued as they both approached the front door to answer.

Morghan's heart raced with anticipation as they opened the door to find both Tabitha and Erich standing there with awkward smiles on their faces.

"Hey, you two! I'm so glad you could make it!" she exclaimed, ushering them into the foyer. If you don't mind, you can remove your shoes. We have some skippy socks for y'all to wear."

Tabitha and Erich remove their shoes and change into the blue and orange fuzzy socks that Morghan handed them.

As the evening unfolded, Tabitha and Erich seemed to get nestled into one another. They seem to be both enjoying the night. Brian was the perfect host, juggling and snacks effortlessly while keeping the night fun. Tabitha couldn't help but notice how Brian's eyes lingered on Morghan when she spoke. He seemed genuinely captivated by her, and for a moment, Tabitha felt a twinge of jealousy. But it wasn't just the way Brian looked at her; it was also the way he cared for her. His gentle teasing, the way he would lean in to whisper funny comments in her ear, and the warmth in his eyes when she looked at him. Tabitha felt a pain of desire mixed with envy. It made her think of everything she missed in Jerrimi Sr.

As the games progressed, Tabitha's mind raced with possibilities. She played the part of being interested in Erich while making small talk and laughing a little too loud at his not-so-funny jokes. Once the men took a break to catch up a bit, Tabitha joined Morghan in the kitchen to refresh the drinks.

"Soo, what do you think about Erich?" Morghan tried to whisper so the men wouldn't hear.

"He seems to be cool! We talked a few times while you were away."

"Really! How did that come about?"

"It seems your friend doesn't know how to take no for an answer. He spotted me pulling into the grocery store parking lot the other day, and he waited for me to go into the store. When I returned to my car, there was a bouquet of flowers with a card that read, I didn't mean to offend you the other night! Please accept my apology."

"He ended it with his phone number, of course. I started to throw it on the ground and drive off, but he caught me on a good day, so I didn't. I waited two more days before I responded to him, then I called."

"Aww," Morghan wailed with a cheesy grin on her face.

"Don't get too happy, though; I said he's cool but nothing else! I'm not ready for anything more."

"I get it Tabitha; I'm just glad you two were able to talk it out. He is a good friend of Brian. They are like brothers."

If he's anything like your husband, then he would be a great catch for someone." That man worships the ground you walk on, girl! He really loves you!"

"Yea, I love him too! Brian is my rock."

On that note, Tabitha takes a sip of her drink and doesn't respond.

"May I use your bathroom?"

"Sure, girl, go ahead."

"Thanks, I remember where it was from last time." Tabitha excuses herself and makes her way to the powder room. Once again, she admires the architecture of the home as she notices what the home looks like before the sun goes down versus when she was there for the barbecue.

She enters the powder room and locks the door. She takes a deep breath, trying to fight the overwhelming feeling of envy that rushed over her. She stood staring into her eyes in the mirror, fighting the tears she felt creeping up. "This is your friend Tabitha; you cannot do anything crazy, she warned herself as she cradled her right thumb back and forth in her fist on her right hand. She flushed the toilet to send a message that she used the bathroom when suddenly she noticed a gray silky head scarf hanging over the bathroom bar. She reached for the scarf with curiosity, wondering if it belonged to Morghan or Brian. Tabitha ran the scarf across her nose to get a whiff of the scent it carried. The scent of the cologne was proof that it obviously belonged to Brian. It must be his wave cap, she thought to herself. Tabitha balled the wave scarf up as small as she possibly could and tucked it inside her bra. Making sure it was well blended and couldn't be seen, then she washed her hands and returned to the games with the others.

"What did I miss?" Tabitha asked as she walked in on the laughter of the room.

"You didn't miss much, just the guys acting foolish as usual," Morghan replied.

"Here, I saved your seat!" Morghan motioned for Tabitha to sit next to her. "We were just about to start another game."

"Great, I'm right on time."

They play a few more games before they decide to call it a night.

"Alright, guys I think I'm going end it with that win," Erich gloats. I came and conquered."

"You the man!" Brian agrees, slapping his hand.

"Yeah, it is getting late, and I have some things to take care of in the morning. I should get going as well."

"Aww, I hate to see you both go!" Morghan and Erich followed them to the front door to see them out. Tabitha, I will call you tomorrow."

"Ok, Morghan, thanks for everything."

"Get home safe, guys."

Brian and Morghan close the door behind them.

Chapter Nine
A Night to Forget

Tabitha pulled into the dimly lit parking lot slowly. Unsure of her surroundings, she parked next to the familiar white vehicle and turned off her car. She looked around to make sure no one was watching as she removed the scarf from under her shirt. She tucked it under the passenger side seat before getting out of the car. Tabitha stepped out into the night air, clutching her purse and wondering if she had made the right decision. Her heart pounded in her chest as she approached the door. Deciding to go through with her choice, she rang the doorbell. The door opened within seconds.

"Hey you! You made it!" Erich smiled, gesturing for Tabitha to enter into his townhome.

"Yup! I made it! Not sure what I'm doing here, but I'm here."

"I just wanted to break away from the chaos to spend a little time with you alone. Have a seat please. Can I get you something to drink?

"Just some water with lemon. Thank you!"

"Sure thing, Erich replies, approaching the bar to get her water.

They chatted for what seemed like hours as conversation flowed easier than when they first met. They exchanged stories, and Tabitha, opening up about her husband and son, explained to Erich why she was so harsh at first.

"I'm really sorry about your lost, Tabitha."

"I really appreciate that, Erich." Tabitha took a moment to really see Erich. She gazed at him, noticing how fine he really was. She had made it a point not to notice his distinguishing features until that moment.

"He really is cute," she thought to herself. He actually resembles Brian a lot. Morghan said they were like brothers, but they could really pass for that. Tabitha gazed at Erich, accepting the charm that had finally drawn her in. His dark skin tone glowed under the soft lighting, highlighting the strong features of his face. His well-groomed beard framed his jawline, adding a hint of sophistication that made her heart race. The low haircut accentuated his sharp cheekbones and the intensity of his dark brown eyes. Tabitha had not noticed anyone other than Jerrimi Sr for the last 7 years. So her feelings were rambling inside of her.

"So, I don't think I ever asked you or Morghan how did you and Brian meet?" Tabitha asked, changing her focus off of Erich's looks.

"We met in freshmen year of college. We both played football in school."

"Ok, that explains the chiseled body." Tabitha thought, again distracted by Erich's broad shoulders and defined arms. Tabitha felt the chemistry arising as Erich moved closer to her on the sofa.

Tabitha, although unsure about the closeness between them, was clear that everything from that moment forward would be wrong. But she didn't stop Erich when he leaned in slowly to kiss her lips. She hesitated for just a moment, considering what was about to happen. Her heart pounding with excitement, she accepts the kiss with no fight in her.

As his hands started to caress her in places she had not felt since Jerrimi's death, Tabitha's thoughts drifted to her husband for a moment. Then she imagined Brian's hands caressing her just as he playfully touched Morghan earlier that night. With each touch, she fantasized more about Brian. Erich slowly unzipped her blouse, making sure his attempt was welcomed. With no objection from Tabitha, he began to unsnap her bra one by one. She, in turn, began to remove his shirt and unzip his pants. Burying her head into his lap felt so wrong, yet it gave her such pleasure that she felt that she was satisfying Brian instead of Erich. The fantasy excited her in unimaginable ways. The explosion of Erich's climax sent a rush of adrenaline through Tabitha, which caused her a premature climax. She lifted her head, realizing what had just happened. As she glanced over at Erich with his head back and eyes closed, she also realized it was not Brian she had just pleasured. Feeling disappointed, Tabitha grabbed her bra off the floor and began to put it back on. The thrill that had just filled her body was quickly replaced with guilt.

'OH MY GOD," OH MY GOD, OH MY GOD, WHAT DID I JUST DO?" Tabitha panics with embarrassment.

"Tabitha, what's wrong?" Erich jumps up, trying to console her.

"THIS WAS WRONG! I SHOULDN'T HAVE COME HERE." She cries, trying to get her blouse on as fast as she can.

"Tabitha, it's ok!"

"NO IT"S NOT! I HAVE TO GO!" She gathers her things and rushes out the door without saying another word to Erich. The thrill of the game night had led her down an unexpected path, and now she had to confront the reality of what she had done. She rushes out the door without turning back to acknowledge Erich.

Tabitha drove beyond the speed limit, trying to make her way home as fast as she could. The knots in her stomach were a mixture of shame and fear of what Erich would tell Brian. "He can't know about this," she murmured to herself. Wiping the fast-rolling tears away with her hand, she took a deep breath, trying to calm the storm inside her mind. As she approached her neighborhood, she slowed down her speed, not wanting to alarm any nosey neighbors. She pulled into the garage and closed it behind her. Looking in the mirror at herself, she spoke,

"Tabitha, what were you thinking? Why would you do that to him? He's not what you want. He could never be Brian.

Stupid, stupid, stupid! You know you have to fix this, right? She asked, wiping one final tear away.

She reached for the scarf under the seat and got out of the car to go inside. She could still taste Erich on her tongue as she made her way straight to the bathroom to wash off all the residue that lingered from her encounter with him. Once she was done, she grabbed her robe along with the gray scarf and went into her spare bedroom. The room was painted in a deep indigo color that resembled a twilight ski. Soft flickering candlelight slightly lit the room. Each corner of the room held its own purpose, with carefully placed items that spoke to her practice of witchcraft. In the center stood a wooden altar with an array of mystical tools and artifacts. A crystal sat in the center of the altar, surrounded by dried herbs and small glass jars filled with colorful powders and oils. Each item had its place, each a component of the spells and rituals she engaged in. A small cauldron sat nearby, its dark metal surface bearing the marks of previous workings, while a silver chalice engraved with intricate designs awaited to be filled with offerings. Tabitha sat down in the rocking chair with the dark velvet throw draped over the arm that her grandmother once used for her workings. She admired the scarf, running it across her face and closing her eyes as she inhaled the familiar scent of her friend's husband. Tabitha thought back to the first time she had used her grandmother's secret weapon of spells. It worked well until it didn't.

Prom 2004

"You look so beautiful Tabitha," her mother and grandmother reassured her as she looked in the mirror one final time.

"Raymond should be here shortly Tabitha; we better get downstairs before he arrives."

Tabitha stood in the mirror, adjusting the delicate straps on her red and black dress, with a slight smile on her face. The dress hugged her curves perfectly. The day had finally arrived. She never thought she'd even attend prom, let alone be going with the star football player.

Tabitha had poured her heart out into planning this night, choosing the perfect dress, and practicing her makeup to a tea, dreaming of the perfect evening with Raymond Lee. The family gathered around the house, waiting to see Tabitha off on her first real date. Everyone's heart pounded with excitement waiting for her date to arrive. Two hours had passed and still no Raymond. Tabitha's date never showed up to pick her up for prom. Devastated as her family began to leave, Tabitha held back tears of embarrassment.

"Oh, Tabitha," her mother cries out with open arms to embrace her. Tabitha turns and runs back up the steps without saying a word. She rushes to her bedroom and slams the door shut. Making sure to lock the door behind her, Tabitha begins to laugh out loud. She could hear everyone knocking at the door, but she refused to respond.

Raymond had not answered any of Tabitha's calls from the day she overheard Chasity and the other girls talking in the bathroom. She wanted to believe that Raymond would not treat her the way that Chasity said he would, but it turned out to be all true. The betrayal stung, which ignited feelings of anger and sadness that spiraled into something more sinister. In her moments of weakness, she had used the spells that her grandmother taught her to her advantage. It was supposed to be a spell to guide Raymond to her, not away. But once he confirmed what Chasity said, it twisted into something darker. In her rage, Tabitha cast a spell to bind Raymond and Chasity together in death. Not expecting it to happen so quickly, Tabitha planned for the prom in hopes that she would see Raymond one last time.

As she lay on her bed pretending to be sad, a vision came to her, a flash of images that made her blood run cold. an accident, a flash of headlights and the screeching of tires. She had seen Raymond and Chasity caught in the last moments that changed everything.

Tabitha rocked in the chair, reminiscing about Raymond and the prom ordeal. The idea that no one ever knew it was her bared an excitement deep down inside. She glanced at the scarf, wondering what she would do to attain Brians heart. In her realm of possibilities, she knew she had to work fast. She gathered each item she would need to use, along with a book of incantations and the scarf. She began to chant the ritual that would take Brian out of Morghan's arms and into hers.

Chapter Ten
Morghan & Brian

"Good morning, babe," Brian awoke, reaching over to caress Morghan's arm. To his surprise, there was just a cold, empty space holder. "Morghan" he called out, assuming she was in the bathroom. There was no answer. He sat up slowly, rubbing his eyes and trying to shake off the tiredness. The house was silent, except for the distant chirping he could here through the window.

A slight panic began to creep in as he walked through the house, trying to find Morghan. It was not like her to leave without saying anything. After checking the deck and the garage with no luck, he picked up his phone, dialing her number with a growing sense of urgency.

"Hey babe," Morghan's voice came through the speaker, unaware of the scare she had just imposed on her husband.

"Where are you"? You just left without telling me," he said, trying to keep his tone light but failing to hide his concern.

"Oh, I just went out for a quick run," she replied, her breath slightly heavier as if she had just stopped running. "I wanted to catch the sunrise! It's really beautiful this time of the morning."

Brian sighed, the tension in his shoulders easing up slightly. "Babe, you could have told me or left a note or something. I woke up, and you were gone! I didn't know what to think!"

"I'm sorry, she said, her voice softening. I didn't mean to worry you. I just wanted to clear my mind and enjoy the quiet. I'll be back soon, I promise."

"Ok then, just be careful," he replied. "I'll be waiting for you."

After hanging up, Brian made his way back to the kitchen to make some coffee. Although the coffee was warm and comforting, his peace was tainted by the unease of Morghan's sudden departure. He couldn't shake that something was off, even if he knew she just needed time to herself.

As he sipped his coffee, his phone buzzed on the counter. It was a text from Erich. Brian opened the message, and it read, "Hey man! We need to talk! Brian quickly typed a response but was interrupted by a call from Erich. He answered, taking another sip of his coffee.

"Hey E! What's up?"

Not much man; I just wanted to check-in.

How are you guys doing after the other night?" Erich's voice sounding warm and genuine.

"We're doing alright. It was nice to have you and Tabitha over. We needed that night of fun, Brian replied, leaning against the counter.

"Yeah, I thought you two were great hosts. Speaking of," his tone shifted. I had an interesting encounter with Tabitha after we left."

Brian felt an instant knot in his stomach. "Oh really? What happened?"

"Well, you know we arrived there together?"

"Well, I saw that y'all came in together; I just assumed you got here at the same time."

"Sort of, kind of! We had spoken a few days before, so we decided to come together. She did drive her car, though. Anyway, we met up at my place after we left there. The night seemed to be going well from my standpoint. I wasn't expecting anything. Well, one thing led into another, and next thing I know, her head was in between my legs."

"Man what!" Brian replied, almost spitting his coffee out.

"Yeah, man, I don't know where that came from, but I was fine with it until she got up and ran out suddenly. I don't know what happened."

Brian's brow furrowed. "Really? Do you think she got embarrassed all of a sudden?"

"I mean, she could have, but I hope she's not angry with me. I didn't ask for that and like I said, I wasn't even expecting anything. I just wanted to get to know her a little. But she ran out of here so quickly that I didn't get to say a word to try to stop her."

"Have you talked to her since?"

"Nope! That's why I wanted to hit you up and see if Morghan has said anything."

"No Morghan has not said a word to me about it. I don't think she's talked to her either since that night."

"Okay, well I guess I will call her to try and smooth things over. I hope she's not regretting anything. I really would still like to spend some time with her."

"Call her and see what she says. You know she is working through grief just as Morghan and I, so it might have been moving too fast for her, and she got overwhelmed. Do you want me to say anything to Morghan or just wait to see how it plays out?"

"Just wait for now. If she hasn't said anything to you, she probably doesn't know anything about it, and the last thing I want to do is embarrass her more."

"Yeah, I get that! Just let me know how it goes."

"I appreciate that. I'll talk to her later today and get back to you."

"Alright Later!"

They hung up, and Brian sat at the kitchen counter in silence, trying to take in everything his friend had just told him. Still sipping on his coffee, he heard the front door open. Morghan's, cheerful voice echoed through the house.

"Guess who's back!" she called out.

"Welcome back, you! Did you enjoy your run and the sunrise?"

"It was amazing! You should have joined me! I feel so much better after that."

"I'm glad!" He replied, standing up to wrap his arms around her. "I'm glad you're back."

"I'm gonna make a smoothie now," she said, breaking away from the embrace to make her way to the sink to wash her hands.

Brian, noticing the way she smiled, did not reach her eyes. "Are you ok, babe?" He asked, feeling a bit concerned.

"Yes, love, I'm fine!

Trying to match her enthusiasm, he couldn't shake the feeling that something was off. Her movements seem to be a bit animated as if she was trying to convince herself of something.

"Did you see anyone else out running?" He asked.

"No, just me and the morning. It felt nice not to have anyone else around."

Her response struck a nerve in Brian, as it was peculiar. Morghan had always loved the company of others, even during her runs.

"Sometimes it's good to disconnect," she said

As she continued making her smoothie, Brian watched, studying her face, searching for the familiar glow he had known so well. But all he saw was an unsettling distance as she was present but not entirely there. Bian couldn't put his finger on it, but he felt deep-seated worry creeping up in his gut.

"Are you sure you're ok? You seem a little different,"

Morghan looked up, tilting her head slightly with a smile. "Different how?"

"I don't know, just …. a bit off, I guess. Like there's something on your mind."

She took a deep breath, adding her ingredients to the blender, 'I'm fine, really. Just processing some things."

Processing what? "You know you can always talk to me about anything, Morghan. You know that!"

"I know, it's just that sometimes I feel like I need to handle things on my own. Like I don't want to burden you with my thoughts."

"Morghan, you could never be a burden to me, we're in this together. Remember? We promised to support each other, no matter what."

Morghan looked up at Brian, her eyes fighting back tears and something else he couldn't quite place.

"I appreciate you! I really do, I just…. I don't want to drag you down into my headspace."

Brian reached out, gently touching her arm, "You're not dragging me down. I want to be there for you. I want to understand what you are feeling."

Morghan hesitated, biting her lip as if she were weighing her words carefully. "It's just…things have changed so much since we lost Amiya. Some days, I feel like I'm floating like I'm not really here. And I thought going for that run would help ground me, but now I feel …. different. I feel like there's this part of me that wants to break free, to escape the pain, and I don't know how."

Brian's heart ached as he listened to his wife express the hurt she was feeling.

"I can understand that you want to escape the pain, but we have to face it together. We have to find a way to get through this together. We can't run away from it."

Morghan nodded in agreement as she reached for his hand. "You're right! I want us to do this together, but it's harder than I thought.

"It's okay Morghan; we can lean on each other when we're feeling weak. That is what love is for."

They hugged and agreed they would lean on one another for help getting through. Brian still couldn't shake the feeling that something still was lingering beneath the surface with Morghan. But at that moment, he decided to let it go.

Chapter Eleven
Tabitha

Tabitha sat at her desk in her home office, trying to focus on the pile-up of client emails that were waiting for her reply, but her mind wandered on several things at once. One was her husband Jerrimi, who's deep voice and contagious laughter she missed so much. The other was her son Jerrimi Jr., which she was struggling each day to move on without. Another was the heaviness of embarrassment she felt from what had taken place almost a week ago at Erich's house and, last but not least, her desire for Brian. Each thought caused a confusing mix of emotions in her head making it terribly hard to pay attention to the email she had forced herself to click on. As she tried to skim over the words in the email, her thoughts drifted back to Brian. She thought of the game night and how he was so attentive to Morghan that night. She imagined him attending to her needs. She looked over to see Brian leaning casually against the doorframe of her office with a flirtatious smile on his face. His presence seemed to push away the feelings of grief she felt about the two Jerrimi's, and the embarrassment about Erich. As he approached her desk, his eyes locked onto hers with an intensity that made her pulse speed up.

"You've been working too hard, Tabitha! He said, his voice smooth and inviting. Why don't you take a break?"

She imagined him reaching out, gently stroking her hair behind her ear, his touch sending a shiver down her spine. The thought of his hands, strong yet gentle, made her heart race.

"Let me help you relax," he continued, his eyes never leaving hers. She found the mischief in his voice to be irresistible. As she reached out to put her hands into his, the moment was shattered by the loud buzz in her air pods. The startle shifted her back into reality. She reached for the phone on the desk to see who was calling. "Erich" is what caller ID revealed.

"I haven't talked to him since I ran out of his house last week," she thought.

She took a deep breath and pressed the answer button.

"Hello"

"Hey, how are you, Tabitha?" Erich spoke on the other end of the line.

"Hi, Erich!" Tabitha voice was a little shaky as she replied.

"I haven't heard from you and wanted to check and see how you were doing."

"Erich, I'm sorry about last week! I never meant for it to go that far, and once I realized what was happening, well, I was embarrassed!"

"Tabitha, no worries! I understand! I apologize for allowing it to get to that point. I never should have taken advantage of your vulnerability. I'm sorry! If it's not too late, can we start over? This time on a real date!"

The silence was so thick; a knife could have cut through the lines, Erich thought before finally Tabitha spoke.

"I would actually like that, Erich!"

"Okay, how about Friday night? I can pick you up if that's ok."

"That's fine! I will text you the address."

"Okay, see you around 7 on Friday."

"Yup, sounds good!

Tabitha ended the call. She blinked, shaking her head to clear the fog of her thoughts. She glanced around the room, making sure her daydream was not real. Then she glanced at the computer with the emails still waiting on her for her confirmation that it was just a fantasy. She smiled and forced herself to focus on the work at hand, but as she began, her thoughts started to linger again.

"I haven't heard from Morghan in a while." She thought, picking up her phone again to scroll through her messages. "I wonder if she's noticed a change in Brian's attentiveness yet" she whispered to herself as she thought about the connotation she spoke over his scarf. "It should be working by now," she thought as she looked at her watch.

She found Morghan's name in her messages and pressed call. The phone rang several times before, finally, a voice answered.

"Hello," a raspy voice spoke.

"May I speak with Morghan?"

"Tabitha, really! Who else would be answering my phone?"

"Morghan, is that you? You sound horrible! Are you ok?"

"I'm feeling a little under the weather." She replied, sounding as if she was shuffling around.

"I'm sorry to hear that! I guess that explains why I haven't heard from you."

"Yeah, I just haven't been feeling like myself since the game night."

"Oh wow! You think you caught something?"

"I'm not sure Tabitha! Possibly!" She said, still shuffling around.

"Are you busy?" Tabitha asked. It sounds like you're running around the house."

"Not really; I'm just looking for my gray scarf so that I can tie my hair up."

"Gray scarf!" Tabitha repeated as she instantly thought of the scarf she had taken from their bathroom, assuming it was Brian's. I remember seeing it in the bathroom when I was there if that's the one you mean."

"Yes, that's it! I can't find it anywhere!"

"I can come over and help you look for it."

"No, it's ok; I don't want to pass my germs off to you. I'll find it! Maybe Brian just moved it without me knowing. I'll ask him when he gets back."

"Oh, Brian is out?" Tabitha asked curiously.

"Yeah, he went to get me some soup for lunch. You know how he's always fussing over me."

"Yeah, I love that about him. I mean, who wouldn't want a man who fusses over their every need?" Tabitha replies nonchalantly.

"I guess you're right! Although, there can be some ups and downs to that sometimes."

"This ungrateful bitch" Tabitha whispers as she mutes and removes the phone from her ear to make certain of what Morghan had just said.

Morghan sighs loudly.

"Do you need me to bring anything over to you Morghan, to help you feel better?" Tabitha offers.

"No, thanks! I think I will be fine. Once Brian gets back from The Soup Bar, I'll eat and rest. He wouldn't have it any other way. I appreciate you calling to check on me, though."

"Ok then, Morghan, I'll call you later this week. Feel better soon!" Tabitha rushes off the phone before Morghan can respond. She grabs her purse and keys off the desk and heads for the door.

"I think I may need some soup for lunch," she smiles and walks out the garage door.

Chapter Twelve
The Soup Bar

The bell above the door of the Soup Bar chimed as Brian pushed through, the warm, savory aromas of simmering broth and fresh-baked bread hitting him instantly. He barely noticed the familiar sounds of clattering bowls and cheerful conversations as his mind was preoccupied with his wife, Morghan. She had been under the weather for the past few days, and her symptoms seemed to be getting worse. He hoped the chicken and wild rice soup would bring her some comfort.

As he scanned the menu overhead, a voice interrupted his thoughts.

"Brian? What are you doing here?"

He turned to see Claudette, Morghan's best friend, standing near the counter with a half-smile on her lips. She was holding a paper cup, probably some of the bar's famous chai tea.

"Hey, Claudette," Brian replied with a nod. "Morghan's not feeling great. I thought I'd get her some soup."

Claudette's expression softened with concern. "Oh no, poor thing. I didn't realize she was that bad. What does she have, the flu?"

"Yeah, probably something like that. She's been in bed for a couple of days now," Brian said, rubbing the back of his neck. "Just trying to keep her comfortable. It's hard to tell if it's the grief of Amiya getting the best of her again or if she is really sick. Either way, I thought maybe some soup would help her feel a bit better."

As they chatted, the bell over the door chimed again, and Brian felt a sudden prickling at the back of his neck. He looked up, and there she was, Tabitha. Her entrance was slow but deliberate. She didn't look around for a table or seem interested in food. Instead, her eyes found Brian almost immediately.

"Brian! What a surprise," Tabitha greeted, her voice airy and filled with a false sweetness.

"Tabitha. Hey." Brian kept his tone polite, but inwardly, he was unsettled. He had seen Tabitha only a few times since Morghan had introduced them, and he felt a little embarrassed for her after finding out what had occurred with Erich. But something about her this time felt off. Morghan seemed to like her, though.

Claudette's eyes drew toward Tabitha, and Brian didn't miss the way her expression changed. He had seen that look before—the protective spark she always got when it came to Morghan. And now that Tabitha had joined them, Claudette's stance shifted a subtle yet noticeable positioning that placed her just slightly closer to Brian.

"How's Morghan doing?" Tabitha asked, her eyes shifting between Claudette and Brian as though she was piecing together something unseen.

"She's... she's not great," Brian said, stepping up to place his order at the counter. "I was just getting her some soup."

"Oh, you poor thing, Brian. You must be so worried about her," Tabitha cooed, her eyes lingering on him in a way that made Claudette subtly shift again.

"Well, it's probably just a cold," he said, offering a tight smile. "Nothing too serious, I hope."

"Still, you must be so exhausted. Taking care of her and everything." Tabitha's voice pretended to offer sympathy, but the undertone was off, something between an invitation and a warning.

Claudette cleared her throat. "Brian's good at taking care of his wife. They're a solid team," she said pointedly, her eyes locking with Tabitha's in a brief, tense moment. Brian hadn't seen Claudette this sharp before, but it was clear she had no patience for Tabitha's presence there.

Tabitha smiled, "I'm sure. Morghan is very lucky to have him."

Just then, Brian's order number was called, cutting through the tension. He stepped to the counter to retrieve the bag of soup. The receipt was folded over the top, and he glanced at it to double-check the order.

That's when he saw it.

"Cilantro?" he muttered under his breath.

Morghan was allergic to cilantro, and not only allergic, but it was also life-threatening and would make her sickness even worse. He waved to the waiter. "Excuse me, is this right? Cilantro in the soup?"

The young server frowned and checked the order on the screen. "Oh, no, I'm so sorry, sir. That was a mistake. I'll fix that for you right away."

As the waiter hurried off, Brian felt a chill slide down his spine. He looked over and caught Tabitha staring at him, it felt more like *through* him. Her eyes followed every movement as if she were absorbing the situation, calculating. He could almost see the gears turning in her mind.

Suddenly, Brian didn't want to be there anymore. He just wanted to get the soup and get home to Morghan. Whatever was going on with Tabitha, it wasn't his concern. His only priority was his wife.

Claudette stepped closer to Brian as if sensing the shift in the atmosphere. "You good?" she asked in a low voice; her eyes drew toward Tabitha again, who was now casually examining the menu board but still listening intently.

"Yeah. Just ready to get home."

The waiter quickly brought the corrected soup, and Brian nodded his thanks. As he turned to leave, Tabitha caught his eye once more.

"Give my best to Morghan," she said sweetly, though the look in her eyes was anything but.

"I will," Brian replied, forcing a smile.

As he left the Soup Bar with Claudette at his side, he couldn't shake the feeling that something wasn't right. Tabitha's presence lingered uncomfortably, and Claudette's growing unease only confirmed it.

Tabitha stood by the counter long after Brian and Claudette had left, her fingers gently grazing the edge of the menu board. She had heard the entire conversation about the cilantro, about Morghan's condition.

She smirked to herself, feeling a surge of satisfaction. *So Morghan's allergic to cilantro?* That was a useful detail, one she could weave into her next plan.

Her initial attempt with the scarf had failed, but now that she knew it belonged to Morghan, she had another angle, one she hadn't expected. Instead of casting her spell on Brian, she would focus on weakening Morghan further. After all, with Morghan out of the picture, Brian would be hers.

All she needed was the right opportunity.

Tabitha's mind raced with possibilities. The next ritual would need to be stronger more precise. She had the scarf; she had the cilantro allergy. Now, it was just a matter of time.

Her phone buzzed with a message filled with work stuff. "I'd better get back!"

Tabitha smiled as she turned to leave, never placing an order.

Brian closed the front door quietly, careful not to let the sound carry through the house. The last thing he wanted was to disturb Morghan, who was resting in the living room. He could hear the faint sound of the television, some documentary she had been watching on and off when she wasn't dozing.

He walked into the living room, and there she was, curled up under a thick, knitted blanket, looking so much smaller than she normally did. The flush of fever had receded from her cheeks, but her exhaustion was still evident in the way her eyes fluttered open when she saw him.

"Hey, babe," she murmured, her voice raspy. "You were gone a while. Everything okay?"

Brian smiled softly, trying to push the unease from the Soup Bar out of his mind. He placed the bag of soup on the coffee table and sat down beside her on the couch, rubbing her leg gently over the blanket.

"Yeah, just a bit of a line. How are you feeling?" he asked, keeping his tone light.

"Like I've been run over by a truck," she said with a weak smile. "But soup might help."

"Here, let me get it for you," Brian said, carefully pulling out the container of soup and handing it to her along with a spoon. As she took the first few sips, he watched her closely, his mind still reeling from the encounter with Tabitha. He needed to tell her, but part of him wondered if he was just overthinking the situation. Still, it felt wrong to keep it from her.

"So," he said casually, "I ran into Claudette at the Soup Bar." Morghan perked up slightly at the mention of her best friend. "Oh? I miss her. We haven't had a talk in a few days."

"She misses you too," Brian said, leaning back against the cushions. "We talked for a bit. She was worried about you. I told her you've been feeling under the weather."

Morghan nodded, but the exhaustion on her face was evident. She sipped her soup in silence for a moment before looking up at him. "Did she ask if I was coming to the event this weekend?"

"Yeah, she did. I told her you'd probably have to see how you're feeling by then."

Morghan nodded, her attention drifting back to her soup. Brian hesitated, then continued. "Oh, and… Tabitha showed up while I was there too."

Morghan's spoon paused mid-air for a second before she resumed eating. "Really? What was she doing there?"

"I don't know. She said it was a coincidence, but…" Brian paused, unsure how to finish that sentence without sounding paranoid. He didn't want to worry Morghan unnecessarily.

"But what?" Morghan prompted, looking at him with faint curiosity.

"I don't know. Something about her just felt... off," he admitted, rubbing the back of his neck. "She asked about you—said she was sorry to hear you weren't feeling well. But the way she looked at me... I don't know; it just gave me a weird vibe."

Morghan's brow furrowed in confusion. "Tabitha?" She shook her head softly. "She's been a good friend to me since we met. I'm sure she's just concerned."

Brian nodded, but that same feeling from earlier gnawed at him. He didn't want to seem like he was accusing Tabitha of anything; he had no proof, after all. Maybe it was just him being overly cautious, or maybe the stress of Morghan's illness was getting to him. Either way, he decided to leave it for now.

"Yeah, you're probably right," he said, his voice nonchalant. "I guess I'm just tired. Long day."

Morghan reached over and squeezed his hand. "You've been great. I don't know what I'd do without you."

Brian smiled down at her, feeling a surge of affection. "You'd be just fine. But I'm not going anywhere."

He settled back into the couch as she continued to eat her soup. They fell into a comfortable silence, with the gentle hum of the TV filling the gaps between their breaths.

But beneath the quiet, something simmered.

As Brian watched his wife, he couldn't help but think back to Tabitha's eyes, how they had lingered on him for just a second too long, the way she had seemed almost pleased to hear about Morghan's illness. It was like she was waiting for something.

I'm just being paranoid, he told himself again, but even as he thought it, he wasn't sure he believed it.

Morghan finished her soup and set the bowl aside, sinking back into the couch with a soft sigh. "That helped a bit," she said, her voice still raspy but a little more at ease.

Brian reached over and gently brushed her hair away from her face. "Good. Get some more rest, okay? You need it."

She nodded, already drifting off again, her head nestled into the cushions. Brian watched her for a moment, then stood and headed for the kitchen to clean up. As he rinsed out the soup container, his mind wandered back to the receipt of the cilantro. It had been such a small thing, but if he hadn't caught it, Morghan would have had an even worse reaction than she was already dealing with.

He dried his hands and returned to the living room. Morghan was asleep, her breathing soft and even. Brian sat back down beside her, his mind still whirling with pieces of conversation, small details that seemed insignificant but gnawed at him, nonetheless.

Why had Tabitha really been at the Soup Bar? Was it really just a coincidence, or was something else going on? And why had she seemed so... interested in him?

As he settled in for the night, Brian pushed the thoughts aside, determined to focus on taking care of Morghan. But the unease lingered like a whisper at the back of his mind.

Chapter Thirteen
Date Night

Tabitha stood in front of her mirror, carefully applying the final touches of lipstick. The deep crimson shade complemented the sleek black dress she had chosen for the evening, the fabric clinging to her curves in all the right places. Her long hair cascaded down her back, and her eyes, intense and calculating, stared back at her reflection as she completed her look.

But despite the effort she had put into her appearance, her mind was far from her reflection or the night ahead.

Tonight, she was supposed to be with Erich, Brian's best friend. But Erich wasn't the one occupying her thoughts. It was *Brian*.

Tabitha's hands stilled for a moment, her mind drifting to the image of him at the Soup Bar earlier that week. His presence had filled the space in a way that only solidified her desire for him. Everything about him, the way he cared for Morghan, the way he carried himself, made her want him more. She had thought the ritual would have him under her spell by now, but her mistake with the scarf had set things back.

Still, she wasn't worried. It was only a matter of time before Brian was hers. Morghan wouldn't be able to hold on much longer, not with the weakening spell still in effect.

Tabitha smiled to herself, pleased with the plan forming in her mind. She just had to be patient. She could play the long game.

A sharp knock at the door pulled her from her thoughts, and she took a deep breath before heading toward it. When she opened the door, there stood Erich, leaning casually against the frame with that easy-going grin that so many women found charming. He was dressed in a crisp button-down and jeans, the perfect combination of casual and polished.

"Wow," he said, his eyes sweeping over her. "You look stunning, Tabitha."

"Thank you," she replied, her smile polite but not reaching her eyes. Erich wasn't bad-looking. In fact, he had the same tall, strong build as Brian, the same confident air. But no matter how many times she tried to convince herself, Erich simply wasn't Brian. He was just a placeholder, someone to keep her occupied until she could have what she truly wanted.

Erich offered his arm, and she took it, feeling the warmth of his skin against hers as they walked to his car. This was a new start from the disaster that happened at their last meeting. He seemed to like her a lot, even though she had bolted from his place after things had gotten a bit too intense. The guilt of thinking about her late husband, Jerrimi, had flooded her at that moment. But now, even that guilt was fading.

Jerrimi was gone. Her son was gone. And the only person who seemed capable of filling that gaping hole in her life was Brian.

As they drove to the restaurant, Erich kept up a steady stream of conversation—talking about work, a new project he was working on, and the latest news from their group of friends. Tabitha responded when necessary, but her mind kept drifting back to Brian, to the scarf, to the way Morghan had looked so pale and fragile the last time she had seen her.

"Are you okay?" Erich asked suddenly, pulling her from her thoughts.

Tabitha blinked, realizing she had barely been paying attention. "Oh, sorry," she said with a slight smile. "I guess I'm just a little tired. It's been a long week."

"Yeah, I get that," Erich said, smiling sympathetically. "But don't worry. Tonight's going to be fun. You'll feel better once we get some food in you."

Tabitha nodded, forcing herself to focus on the present. Erich was being sweet, and she needed to appear at least interested. He had no idea that she was merely playing a game, keeping him close for now until she could get closer to Brian.

They arrived at the restaurant, a cozy little Italian place with dim lighting and intimate booths. Erich had chosen well—somewhere that would allow for quiet conversation and a comfortable atmosphere. The waiter seated them quickly, and soon enough, they were sipping wine and looking over the menu.

Throughout dinner, Erich was his usual charming self. He told stories that made her laugh, asked questions about her day, and genuinely seemed interested in her life. For anyone watching, they probably looked like the perfect couple, two people thoroughly enjoying each other's company.

But Tabitha's thoughts were miles away. Every time Erich leaned in closer or reached for her hand, her mind conjured an image of Brian doing the same. She imagined what it would be like to sit across from *him* at this table, to feel *his* hand resting on hers.

At one point, Erich was telling a story about a camping trip he and Brian had taken years ago. He was laughing about some ridiculous situation they'd gotten themselves into, but Tabitha only heard one thing: Brian's name. It sent a thrill through her every time Erich mentioned him.

The main course arrived with pasta for Erich, a delicate seafood dish for her, and they ate quietly for a moment. But even as she took a bite, her mind wandered. She thought of the scarf again, sitting on her altar at home. She had planned to redo the ritual soon, this time with the right intention.

Brian would come to her. He had to.

By the time dessert came around, Erich had finally noticed her distraction. He set his fork down and looked at her seriously. "Tabitha, you seem... distant tonight. Is everything okay?"

She blinked and forced a smile, pushing her plate aside. "No, no, I'm fine. Like I said, it's just been a long week."

Erich studied her for a moment as if trying to decide whether or not to believe her. Then, his expression softened, and he reached across the table to take her hand. "If something's bothering you, you can talk to me, you know. I'm here for you."

For a second, she felt a pang of guilt. Erich really did like her. He was trying, genuinely trying to make this work between them. But Tabitha didn't want him. She wanted someone else, someone who wasn't his best friend.

She swallowed, trying to pull herself back into the moment. But the image of Brian and Morghan together clouded her mind, making it impossible to focus.

"Thank you, Brian," she whispered, the words slipping out before she even realized what she had said.

There was a long, heavy silence. Tabitha froze, her eyes widening as her mind caught up with her mouth. Erich's grip on her hand tightened, then slowly released as he pulled back, his face going pale.

"Did you just...?" he began, his voice barely above a whisper.

She stared at him, panic flooding her. "Erich, I'm so sorry. I didn't—"

"No, you did," he said, his voice firmer now. He sat back in his chair, disbelief etched across his features. "You called me Brian."

Tabitha opened her mouth to explain, to say *something* that would make it better, but nothing came out. There was nothing she could say. The truth was written all over her face.

Erich shook his head, his expression hardening. "You've been thinking about him this whole time, haven't you? This entire night... you've been thinking about Brian."

"Erich, I"

"I don't want to hear it," he snapped, standing abruptly from the table. "You should've just been honest with me. If you're not interested, don't string me along like this."

Tabitha watched him storm off, guilt and frustration warring inside her. She hadn't meant to let Brian's name slip; it had just happened. But now that it had, there was no undoing it.

She sat there, staring at the empty chair across from her, feeling the weight of her own actions sinking in.

But as the minutes passed, and the restaurant buzzed around her, something shifted in her mind. Erich didn't matter. This tonight didn't matter.

The only thing that mattered was Brian. And she wasn't giving up on him. Not now. Not ever.

Chapter Fourteen
Blinded by Loss

The morning sun filtered through the curtains, shining a bright natural light over the living room as Morghan stood by the window, looking out into the street. She still felt weak, the sickness that had clung to her for days now refusing to let go. But she was tired of being confined to the house, tired of resting, tired of the weight of grief pressing on her chest every time she closed her eyes.

She had to get out. She had to do *something*.

Brian was in the kitchen, making coffee. She could hear the soft clink of mugs and the gentle hum of the coffee maker as it brewed. She knew he'd try to stop her, but she had made up her mind.

Morghan inhaled deeply, trying to summon what little strength she had left. Her thoughts drifted to Amiya Reign, their daughter. Ever since she had fallen sick, her grief over losing Amiya had resurfaced in ways that left her feeling hollow. The loss had always been there, lingering in the background, but lately, it had become almost unbearable again.

She needed to talk to someone who understood. Someone who knew what it was like to lose a child. And that someone was Tabitha.

Despite Brian's concerns, Tabitha had been a comfort to Morghan in ways few others could be. The shared pain of losing a loved one and the mutual understanding of the emptiness that loss created were things only someone like Tabitha could understand.

She turned from the window just as Brian entered the room, holding a steaming mug of coffee.

"You look like you're thinking about something," he said, eyeing her cautiously. "How are you feeling?"

Morghan sighed and sat down on the couch. "I'm still tired, but... I need to get out of the house, Brian. I can't sit here anymore."

Brian frowned, setting the coffee down on the table in front of her. "You're still not fully better. I don't think it's a good idea for you to be going out just yet."

"I know," she said softly, her voice tinged with frustration. "But I have to. I feel trapped here, and it's making everything worse. I've been thinking about Amiya... a lot."

At the mention of their daughter's name, Brian's expression softened, but the worry in his eyes remained. He sat beside her, reaching for her hand. "I get that. I miss her too, every day. But I don't want you pushing yourself too hard while you're still recovering."

Morghan's fingers tightened around his, her eyes pleading with him to understand. "That's why I need to go see Tabitha."

Brian's face fell, his brow furrowing. "Tabitha? You're thinking of going to see *her*?"

"Yes." Morghan took a deep breath, knowing how he felt about Tabitha. He had been uneasy around her ever since they first met. She had tried to reassure him that Tabitha was harmless, just another grieving soul like herself, but Brian had never quite warmed to her. "She's the only person who understands. She's lost her husband and her son. We've bonded over that. I just... I need to talk to her."

Brian pulled his hand back, his jaw tightening. "I don't like this, Morghan. I don't trust her."

"Why not?" she asked, her voice rising slightly in defense. "She's been nothing but kind to me. I know you've got some weird feelings about her, but she's going through her own pain. Just like me."

Brian ran a hand through his hair, clearly struggling with what to say. He wasn't the type to come out and say that Tabitha was making him uncomfortable, but his concerns had been growing ever since that encounter at the Soup Bar. There was something about the way Tabitha had looked at him, something he couldn't shake.

"I don't know," he said finally, his voice low. "There's just something about her that I can't put my finger on. It's like... she's always too close. Too interested."

Morghan's expression softened, but her resolve remained firm. "She's been a good friend to me, Brian. I know she can be a little... intense, but she's hurting just like we are. I need to talk to her about Amiya."

Brian's heart clenched at the mention of their daughter again. He hated seeing Morghan like this, torn between her illness and her grief. He wanted to be the one to help her through it, but he knew that her connection with Tabitha was something he couldn't replace. Still, the idea of her going to see Tabitha now when she was still so vulnerable, made his stomach twist.

"I just wish you'd wait until you're feeling better," he said, his voice softer now. "Give it a few more days. You need to rest."

Morghan shook her head. "I can't, Brian. I need to go now while I still have the strength to. The grief, it's." She paused, struggling to find the words. "It's been worse since I've been sick. Like I'm losing her all over again. I don't expect you to understand fully, but Tabitha... she gets it."

Brian's shoulders sagged, knowing he wasn't going to win this one. He had seen that look in her eyes before she had already made up her mind.

"Okay," he said finally, though his voice was reluctant. "But promise me you'll take it easy. Don't push yourself too hard."

"I promise," she said, offering him a small, grateful smile.

Brian watched her stand and gather her things, an uneasy feeling settling in the pit of his stomach. He didn't want to let her go. He didn't want her anywhere near Tabitha. But what could he say? Morghan needed this, and he didn't want to be the one standing in her way.

As she slipped on her shoes and grabbed her denim jacket, she turned to look at him, her eyes soft with emotion. "I'll be back soon," she promised, leaning down to kiss his cheek. "Don't worry about me. I'll be fine."

Brian forced a smile, his hand brushing hers as she walked toward the door. "I love you."

"I love you too," she whispered before closing the door behind her.

As soon as the door clicked shut, Brian sat back down on the couch, his mind racing. Something didn't feel right. Maybe it was just his imagination, but the more time Morghan spent with Tabitha, the more uneasy he felt. And now, with Morghan still so sick and fragile, the worry gnawed at him like a dark shadow creeping in from the corners of his mind.

He stared at the door for a long moment, resisting the urge to go after her. He had to trust her. He had to let her do this. But deep down, he couldn't shake the feeling that something was about to go very wrong.

Morghan parked the car outside Tabitha's house on the street. She got out slowly and walked the familiar path up the driveway to Tabitha's house, each step feeling heavier than the last. Her body was still weak, but her heart was heavy with the need to talk about Amiya, to share the pain that had been clawing at her soul since her illness had resurfaced her grief.

When she reached Tabitha's doorstep, she hesitated for a moment before knocking. The door opened almost immediately as if Tabitha had been waiting for her.

"Morghan," Tabitha greeted, her voice warm and soothing. "I'm so glad you came. Come in, come in."

Morghan smiled weakly, stepping inside the house that had become familiar over the past few months. The scent of burning sage filled the air, and the soft hum of calming music played in the background. Tabitha had a way of making everything feel so serene, so safe.

But as she stepped further inside, Morghan couldn't help but notice the lingering tension in her own chest, the same tension that had been building for days. Something was off, but she couldn't quite place it.

"How are you feeling?" Tabitha asked, leading her to the couch. "I know you've been sick. You look pale."

"I'm... better, I think," Morghan replied, though she wasn't sure she believed it. "But I've been thinking about Amiya a lot. I needed to talk to someone who understands."

Tabitha's eyes softened with sympathy, her hand resting gently on Morghan's arm. "Of course. I'm here for you, always. You know that."

Morghan nodded, but the unease that had been nagging at her since the moment she left her house refused to fade. Something about this moment, this conversation, felt different.

But for now, she pushed the feeling aside, allowing herself to be comforted by the only person who truly knew the depths of her pain.

Chapter Fifteen
Warning Signs

Brian sat on the couch, staring at the blank TV screen, a gnawing pit of anxiety forming in his stomach. He couldn't shake the feeling that something was wrong, something just out of reach. The fact that Morghan had gone to see Tabitha *against his wishes* made the anxiety even worse. He trusted his wife; of course, he did, but there was something about Tabitha that had always unsettled him.

His thoughts were interrupted by the sharp buzz of his phone vibrating on the coffee table. He leaned forward, grabbing it. The caller ID flashed *Erich*.

Brian swiped to answer. "Hey, man. What's up?"

There was a pause on the other end, and Brian could hear the hesitation in Erich's voice when he finally spoke. "Brian, I've been meaning to talk to you about something. It's... about Tabitha."

The mention of her name immediately sent a chill down Brian's spine. He leaned back, the tension in his shoulders tightening. "What about her?"

"Look, I waited a few days to cool off because I didn't want to say anything I might regret," Erich said, his voice low and steady. "But I think you need to know this."

Brian's heart rate picked up, his fingers gripping the phone tightly. "Know what? What happened?"

Erich exhaled, clearly still frustrated by whatever had transpired. "We went on a date a few nights ago, and everything seemed fine at first. We were having dinner, talking like usual, but she was... off. Distant. I could tell her mind wasn't really on me. She was distracted the whole night, but I didn't push it because I figured she was dealing with her own stuff. You know, the grief and all."

Brian's gut tightened. He had been noticing the same thing about Tabitha—something was always *off* with her. He didn't like the way she hovered around them, especially around him.

"Then, at the end of the date," Erich continued, his voice growing more agitated, "she called me *Brian.*"

Brian froze, his breath catching in his throat. "Wait... what?"

"Yeah, man," Erich said, frustration clear in his tone. "We were sitting there, having dessert, and she looked right at me and said, 'Thank you, Brian.' Like she wasn't even aware of it, I couldn't believe it."

Brian's mind raced. The fact that Tabitha had been thinking about *him* while on a date with Erich was alarming, to say the least. But the fact that she had *said his name*? That made his skin crawl.

"Erich," Brian said slowly, trying to make sense of it all. "Did she say why she called you that?"

"No," Erich replied, his voice stiff with anger. "She tried to backtrack, apologized, said it was a slip-up or whatever, but I knew better. The whole time, she was thinking about you. It wasn't a mistake."

Brian stood up from the couch, pacing the living room as the dread that had been simmering all morning finally started to boil over. His mind immediately went to Morghan. She was *with* Tabitha right now, at her house, alone.

"Brian, I don't know what's going on with her," Erich continued, clearly sensing the gravity of the situation. "But I figured you should know. Something's not right with Tabitha. She's... obsessed with you."

Brian stopped pacing, his heart thudding painfully in his chest. Erich was right. This was more than just an uneasy feeling. Tabitha had crossed a line, and now Morghan, his sick, vulnerable wife, was alone with her.

"Morghan went to see Tabitha," Brian said abruptly, his voice tight. "She's there right now."

"What?!" Erich sounded alarmed now. "Brian, you need to get her out of there. I don't trust Tabitha, and after what she did on our date... there's no telling what she's capable of."

"I know," Brian muttered, already dialing Morghan's number as he grabbed his keys from the kitchen counter. The phone rang and rang, but there was no answer.

"Come on, Morghan," he muttered under his breath, pacing toward the front door as he dialed again. Still nothing.

His stomach twisted with fear. Why wasn't she answering?

"She's not picking up," Brian said to Erich, his voice tight with panic.

"Jesus, Brian, you need to go there. Now."

Brian didn't need to be told twice. "I'm going; send me the address," he said quickly, hanging up and rushing out the door. His heart pounded in his chest as he unlocked the car and jumped inside, his mind racing with a thousand worst-case scenarios.

As he sped down the streets toward Tabitha's house, Brian dialed Morghan again, praying she would answer. The phone rang again, but each unanswered ring felt like another needle of fear piercing through his gut.

"Pick up, pick up..." he whispered to himself, his knuckles white as he gripped the steering wheel. But there was nothing—just voicemail again.

The unease that had been gnawing at him all morning had now become full-blown terror. Something was wrong. He could feel it deep in his bones.

He pressed the pedal harder, weaving through the traffic as his mind replayed the events of the past few weeks. The strange looks from Tabitha, her presence at the Soup Bar, the scarf that Morghan had been searching for ever since Tabitha had come to their BBQ. And now this calling Erich by his name, the obsession, the stalking.

Tabitha wasn't just unstable. She was dangerous.

As he neared Tabitha's house, Brian's pulse quickened. He had to get to Morghan, had to make sure she was safe.

Pulling up to the curb in front of Tabitha's house, he jumped out of the car, not even bothering to turn off the engine. He raced up the front steps, his heart hammering in his chest as he pounded on the door.

"Morghan!" he yelled, his voice cracking with desperation. "Morghan, open the door!"

There was no answer, and the silence only made his fear grow worse. He pounded on the door again, harder this time. "Tabitha! Open the door!"

Still nothing.

Brian's mind raced, and without thinking, he tried the doorknob. It was unlocked. He pushed it open, stepping into the dimly lit house, the scent of sage hitting him like a wall.

"Morghan?" he called, his voice shaky as he ventured further into the house. His eyes scanned the room, his heart thudding in his ears.

The house was eerily quiet, and the oppressive silence made every hair on his body stand on end.

"Tabitha?" Brian called again, but his voice barely carried.

As he moved further into the house, his dread deepened. He had to find Morghan. He had to get her out of here before it was too late.

Chapter Sixteen
Poisoned by Trust

Morghan sat across from Tabitha, the atmosphere deceptively calm. They had been talking for nearly an hour about grief, loss, and the never-ending ache of losing a child. It felt familiar and comforting, but beneath the surface, something was lurking. Morghan couldn't put her finger on it, but the knot of unease that had formed in her stomach refused to go away.

She felt tired, her body still weak from the illness that had plagued her for days. She had come here hoping to find some solace in Tabitha's shared pain, but now that she was here, she only felt drained.

"I should get going," Morghan said softly, shifting on the couch. "Brian will worry if I'm gone too long."

Tabitha nodded, her smile never quite reaching her eyes. "Of course, I understand. You need to rest."

Morghan stood slowly, her legs shaky beneath her, and began gathering her things. "Could I get some water for the road?" she asked, her voice slightly strained.

"Of course," Tabitha replied smoothly, already moving toward the kitchen. "I've only got water with some mint leaves in it. I hope that's okay?"

Morghan hesitated for a brief second. She didn't particularly like flavored water, but she was too tired to care. "Yeah, that's fine. I just need something to sip on while I drive."

Tabitha returned a moment later with a cold plastic cup of water with a straw in it, with condensation beading on the plastic. She handed it to Morghan, her smile never wavering. "Here you go. Be careful on the road, okay?"

Morghan nodded, offering a faint smile in return. "Thanks. I'll see you soon."

She didn't notice the way Tabitha's eyes lingered on her as she walked out the door or the slight hint of satisfaction that crossed her face as Morghan sat down in the driver's seat and took a sip. The minty taste was refreshing, and as Morghan buckled herself into her car, she took another long sip, grateful for the coolness on her throat.

The drive home started off quietly, the familiar streets blurring together in her peripheral vision as she focused on the road. But not even ten minutes in, something shifted.

It started with a slight tingling in her throat, something she barely registered at first. She brushed it off, thinking it was just the remnants of the cold she was still shaking off. But as the tingling grew, turning into a sharp constriction, her eyes widened in sudden fear.

Her breath hitched, and she coughed, trying to clear her throat, but it only made things worse. Panic surged through her as the familiar, terrifying sensation of her throat closing up gripped her body.

Oh God… cilantro.

Her hands scrambled for the bottle, her eyes darting to the label as she tried to focus. Her mind raced, replaying the moment when Tabitha had mentioned mint leaves, but she knew *this wasn't mint*. She could feel it now, the unmistakable reaction her body always had to cilantro.

Her breath came in short, ragged gasps as her vision blurred. She needed her EpiPen *now*.

With trembling hands, she fumbled through her bag, her fingers barely able to grasp the small case containing the lifesaving injector. But just as her hand closed around it, a wave of dizziness hit her, and the steering wheel jerked to the side.

The car veered off the road, her vision swimming as she lost control. The world spun in a chaotic blur of lights and trees, the screeching of tires filling her ears before the sickening crash came.

Everything went black.

Brian's knuckles were white as he pounded on Tabitha's front door, his heart thudding in his chest. He had stormed through the house minutes earlier, searching for Morghan in every room, but there had been no sign of her.

Tabitha appeared from the back of the house, her expression calm, almost serene. "Brian," she greeted, her voice soft, "what are you doing here?"

"Where's Morghan?" Brian demanded, his voice shaking with fear. "She's not answering her phone."

"She left not too long ago," Tabitha said casually, wiping her hands on a towel as if she had been in the middle of something mundane. "She wasn't feeling great, so she headed home. Did something happen?"

Brian's blood ran cold. "What do you mean she left? She's not picking up. She should be home by now."

Tabitha's eyes blinked briefly, something unreadable passing over her face. "I'm sure she's fine," she said, her voice soothing. "Maybe she just didn't hear her phone."

Brian didn't respond. His instincts were screaming at him now, every nerve on edge. He turned and rushed back outside, dialing Morghan's number again as he ran. Still no answer. His heart raced as he climbed into his car, speeding off in the direction of the route Morghan would have taken home.

He drove with his eyes scanning the roadsides, his hands trembling as fear gnawed at him. And then, as he rounded a bend, his breath caught in his throat.

There, off the side of the road, was Morghan's car crashed into a tree, the front end crumpled and smoke rising faintly from the engine.

"No, no, no..." Brian's voice cracked as he skidded to a stop, throwing the car into the park and running toward the wreckage. His heart pounded in his ears, each step feeling like it took an eternity as he raced toward the car.

"Morghan!" he screamed, his voice hoarse as he reached the driver's side door. Her body was slumped over the steering wheel, unconscious, her skin pale and her breath shallow.

Without hesitation, Brian ripped open the door and unbuckled her seatbelt, gently pulling her out of the car and laying her on the ground. His hands shook as he reached for the EpiPen in her hand, which had fallen to her side in the crash. He injected her quickly, praying it wasn't too late.

"Come on, baby," he whispered, his voice breaking. "Please, wake up. Please."

For a few agonizing moments, nothing happened. The world seemed to stand still, the silence pressing in on him as he knelt beside her, willing her to breathe.

And then, finally, a gasp.

Morghan's eyes fluttered open, her breaths coming in shallow, ragged bursts. Relief washed over Brian so intensely that his body shook with it. He leaned over her, brushing the hair away from her face as tears filled his eyes.

"Thank God," he whispered, pressing his forehead to hers. "You're okay. You're okay."

But as he held her, a chilling thought crept into his mind— one that made his blood run cold.

This wasn't an accident.

This was *Tabitha*.

Brian's jaw clenched as the realization hit him, his grip tightening protectively around Morghan. He would never let Tabitha near her again. Brian held Morghan close for a moment longer, his heart pounding against his ribs, before the urgency of the situation snapped him back into action. He fumbled for his phone, his fingers shaking as he dialed 911.

"911, what's your emergency?" the dispatcher's voice was calm and professional, but to Brian, it felt like he was moving through a haze.

"My wife has had an allergic reaction. Her throat was closing up—she crashed the car. We're on Maple and Elm, just past the bend. Please send an ambulance!" His voice was strained, panic woven through every word.

"Help is on the way. Stay with her. Is she breathing?"

Brian glanced down at Morghan, her breathing ragged but steady, the rise and fall of her chest shallow. "Yes, but it's weak. I gave her the EpiPen, but she needs help; she's not out of the woods yet."

"Stay calm, sir. The paramedics are on their way. Do not move her unless the car is in immediate danger."

Brian was already a step ahead of that. The car was wrecked, but it wasn't smoking anymore, and there didn't seem to be any imminent threat. Still, the sight of the crumpled metal and broken glass made his stomach churn.

He knelt beside Morghan, brushing her hair away from her face, his thumb gently tracing the outline of her cheek. Her eyes fluttered, struggling to stay open, and every few seconds, a sharp breath would escape her lips.

"It's okay," Brian whispered, more to himself than to her. "Help's coming. You're going to be fine."

The minutes felt like hours. The distant sound of sirens grew louder, cutting through the tension, until finally, the flashing lights of an ambulance appeared around the bend. Brian waved them down frantically as they pulled up beside the wreck.

The paramedics jumped out of the vehicle, moving swiftly toward Morghan. They gently but efficiently took over, checking her vitals and asking Brian rapid-fire questions about what had happened, what her allergies were, and how long ago she had taken the EpiPen.

"She's allergic to cilantro," Brian explained, his voice cracking slightly as he recounted the events. "She drank something with it, and her throat started closing up. She's had the EpiPen, but..."

The paramedics nodded, working quickly to stabilize her and load her onto a stretcher. One of them looked up at Brian as they prepared to lift Morghan into the ambulance. "We'll get her to the hospital. You can ride with us if you want."

Brian didn't hesitate. He climbed into the ambulance beside his wife, gripping her hand as the paramedics began their work, attaching monitors checking her oxygen levels. Her breathing was still shallow, but the EpiPen seemed to be helping just not fast enough for Brian's peace of mind.

The drive to the hospital was a blur. Brian barely registered the motion of the ambulance or the hurried movements of the paramedics. All he could focus on was Morghan's face, pale and drawn, her breaths still labored. His mind raced with what had happened, how close he had come to losing her.

How close *Tabitha* had come to taking her away.

As the ambulance pulled into the emergency bay, the doors flew open, and more medical staff rushed to meet them. Morghan was whisked away to be evaluated further, and Brian was left standing at the entrance to the ER, his chest heaving as adrenaline surged through his veins.

He followed the doctors inside, though they guided him to the waiting area, assuring him they would take good care of her. But the moment they wheeled Morghan out of sight, the room closed in on him.

The weight of everything that had just happened crashed down on him all at once. He collapsed into a chair, his hands still trembling, his mind spinning. She was alive; she was safe— for now. But the thought of how close he had come to losing her because of Tabitha's twisted obsession gnawed at him like a relentless storm.

He took out his phone and texted Erich.

Brian: "We're at the hospital. Morghan had an allergic reaction. She crashed the car. It was Tabitha. I'm sure of it."

The response came quickly.

Erich: "What the hell? I'm on my way."

Brian's jaw clenched. Tabitha had crossed a line that could never be uncrossed. Whatever had happened on that date with Erich, whatever feelings she had for him—none of it mattered anymore. Morghan's safety was his priority. And whatever game Tabitha was playing, it was about to come to an end.

As he sat in the waiting room, his fists clenched, Brian made a silent vow: he would protect Morghan at any cost.

He wouldn't let Tabitha win.

A nurse appeared from the hallway, interrupting his thoughts. "Mr. Alexander?"

Brian stood up quickly, his heart in his throat. "Yes, that's me. How's my wife?"

"She's stable," the nurse said, offering him a reassuring smile. "The EpiPen helped, and we've given her some additional medication to help with the reaction. She'll need to stay for observation for a while, but she's awake now."

The relief that washed over him was so overwhelming that he had to steady himself against the nearby wall. "Thank you," he whispered, his voice thick with emotion.

"She's asking for you. You can see her now."

Brian followed the nurse down the hallway, his legs weak but his determination strong. When he entered the room, he saw Morghan lying in the hospital bed, pale but conscious, her eyes fluttering open when she heard him come in.

"Brian..." she whispered, her voice hoarse.

He rushed to her side, taking her hand in his and kissing her knuckles gently. "Hey, I'm here. You're okay. You're safe now."

Morghan smiled weakly, though the confusion in her eyes was clear. "I don't know what happened. The water... I thought it was just mint, but... I think it had cilantro."

Brian's chest tightened. He nodded, not wanting to burden her with the full weight of his suspicions just yet. "We'll talk about it later. Right now, just rest. You're going to be okay."

But inside, Brian's mind was already racing, forming the next steps. Tabitha had made her move, and now it was his turn.

Chapter Seventeen
Plan Initiated

Claudette paced across her living room, her heart pounding as she replayed the conversation she had just had with Brian. The news of Morghan's accident had shaken her to the core. She had always been suspicious of Tabitha, her gut telling her something was off about that woman. But now it was clear—Tabitha had crossed a line, one that couldn't be ignored.

Claudette grabbed her phone and quickly dialed Brian's number again. It rang twice before he picked up.

"Brian," she said urgently, "how's Morghan? I can't believe this happened."

"She's stable, but she's still shaken," Brian replied, his voice rough with exhaustion. "It was Tabitha, Claudette. I'm sure of it. The water had cilantro in it, and she gave it to Morghan, knowing she's allergic."

Claudette felt her stomach drop. She had always hated how close Morghan had gotten to Tabitha. The woman had wormed her way into their lives with her grief-stricken story and her quiet intensity. Morghan had seen a kindred spirit in her, but Claudette had seen something else—something darker.

"We need to do something about her," Claudette said, her voice hardening. "She can't get away with this."

Brian was silent for a moment on the other end of the line, but Claudette could hear the frustration simmering beneath the surface.

"I know," he finally said. "But what can we do? I don't have any proof. I can't exactly go to the police and tell them I *think* she tried to kill my wife."

Claudette stopped pacing and leaned against the kitchen counter, her mind racing. Tabitha had been growing bolder—more dangerous. If they didn't act soon, there was no telling what she might do next.

"I don't know," Claudette admitted, her voice lowering. "But we can't just sit back and wait for her to make her next move. We need to make her pay."

Brian sighed, the sound of weariness in his voice apparent. "You're right. But she's smart. She's been careful not to leave a trail. We need a plan."

Claudette's eyes narrowed as she thought about how to deal with someone like Tabitha. She knew she couldn't take the direct approach—Tabitha was slippery, always one step ahead. But there had to be a way to expose her, to force her hand. Claudette had connections and friends who were good at digging up dirt. If Tabitha had any skeletons in her closet, Claudette was determined to find them.

"Okay," Claudette said, her mind already working through possibilities. "Let's start by digging into her past. She's been in the support group for what, six months? But I don't know anything about her before that. There's got to be something."

Brian agreed, though his voice carried a weight of worry. "Yeah, but be careful. There's something else you should know."

"What is it?" Claudette asked, sensing the hesitation in his voice.

"I think Tabitha's obsessed with me," Brian admitted, his voice low, almost as if saying it aloud made it real. "Erich went on a date with her a few days ago, and she accidentally called him *Brian.* He said she seemed distracted the whole night like she wasn't even interested in him."

Claudette's breath caught in her throat. That was worse than she thought. This wasn't just about Morghan anymore— Tabitha had fixated on Brian, and that made her dangerous in a whole new way.

"That woman's got problems," Claudette muttered, her voice hardening with anger. "We're going to have to be smart about this."

"Yeah," Brian said, his tone grim. "But be careful. I don't trust her, and there's something else... something I haven't told you."

Claudette raised an eyebrow. "What?"

"Morghan's been missing a scarf," Brian said, his voice strained. "The one she lost after Tabitha came over for the BBQ. She keeps asking about it, and I think... I think Tabitha took it. But why? I have no idea."

Claudette's stomach twisted as a strange sense of fear settled over her. She couldn't shake the feeling that there was more to this than just obsession or jealousy. The idea of Tabitha taking a scarf, of all things, didn't sit right with her. It felt deliberate, purposeful.

"That's odd," Claudette said slowly, her mind working through the pieces. "Why would she take something so personal?"

"I don't know," Brian said, frustration clear in his voice. "But whatever she's doing, I'm not going to let her hurt Morghan again."

Claudette nodded, even though Brian couldn't see her. "Okay. I'll start looking into her background. You stay close to Morghan, and don't let Tabitha near her."

"Got it."

They hung up, and Claudette stood in the silence of her kitchen, staring out the window into the darkening evening. The unease in her gut grew, a gnawing feeling that something terrible was coming. She wasn't sure how, but Tabitha had to be stopped. Claudette would do whatever it took, but she had a growing suspicion that they were dealing with something far darker than a simple obsession.

Tabitha wasn't just cunning. She was dangerous. And if Claudette's gut was right, she was involved in something much worse than they had imagined.

Meanwhile, back at Tabitha's house, the air was thick with the smell of burning sage. The small room in which she had set up her altar was dimly lit, the candles casting flickering shadows on the walls. Tabitha sat cross-legged in front of the small shrine she had built, her eyes closed as she muttered incantations under her breath.

In her hands was the scarf she had taken from Morghan's home. She held it tightly, her fingers brushing over the fabric as she chanted, her voice growing stronger with each passing second.

The ritual had not gone as planned. The scarf wasn't Brian's; it had been Morghan's. And because of that, the spell meant to bind Brian to her had instead begun to weaken Morghan, making her ill and draining her strength. It was a mistake, but one that could be corrected.

As she continued chanting, her mind filled with images of Brian. He belonged to her; she knew it. Morghan had only been an obstacle, something that had to be removed so that she and Brian could be together. The magic would work; she just needed more time.

A faint smile crossed Tabitha's lips as she visualized Brian standing beside her, Morghan out of the picture for good. The scarf would help with that. The ritual would bind them together, and nothing, not Brian's resistance, not Morghan's strength, could stop it.

Her eyes snapped open, the flicker of the candles glaring a haunting glow across her face.

The game had only just begun.

And Claudette, Brian, and Morghan had no idea what they were up against.

Chapter Eighteen
The Past Unraveled

Claudette sat hunched over her desk, the low hum of her laptop the only sound breaking the heavy silence in the room. Claudette had been consumed with finding out the truth about Tabitha.

Something wasn't right. Claudette's gut told her that Tabitha's past held secrets, and she was determined to uncover them. After hours of digging, she stumbled upon a news article from years ago that made her heart drop.

The headline read: "Tragic Accident Claims Father and Son Moving to Texas."

Her fingers hovered over the mouse as she clicked on the article, her heart thudding in her chest. The names were familiar. Jerrimi Sr. and Jerrimi Jr.—Tabitha's husband and son.

They had been on their way to Texas from Lafitte, Louisiana, the article said, moving for Tabitha's new job. The truck they were driving had crashed late at night on a desolate highway. There were no witnesses, no signs of foul play. Just a tragic accident.

Claudette's brow lifted as she scrolled through the article, but something about it felt off. She couldn't explain it, but the words on the screen seemed to lack the closure that usually accompanied a tragedy like this. There were too many unanswered questions.

Her eyes darted to a small, buried detail near the end of the article one that made her heart skip a beat.

Jerrimi Sr. had spoken to Tabitha the night before the accident. According to the report, it said after speaking with his wife, he had mentioned they needed to "talk about something" when he got there. She never got to see what it was.

Claudette leaned back in her chair, her mind racing. *What did he need to talk to her about?* And why hadn't they talked about it?

Her fingers flew across the keyboard, searching for anything that could shed light on the cryptic statement. She found a few scattered forums and old social media posts that referenced Tabitha's past but nothing substantial. That was until she stumbled across an obscure blog post from someone in Lafitte—someone who remembered the story of a high school tragedy that had haunted the small town for years.

The blog post detailed an accident that had occurred many years ago. A high school football player and his girlfriend had died on the way to prom, their car flipping off a narrow road on the way to prom. The boy, it was rumored, had been seeing another girl behind his girlfriend's back. That girl? Tabitha.

Claudette's blood ran cold as she read further. The post went on to describe Tabitha as a quiet, strange girl, one who had always kept to herself. But after the football player's death, whispers had started to circulate. People said she had been obsessed with him, that she had learned dark magic from her grandmother, who was known in town for her peculiar rituals.

As the blog recounted, there were rumors that Tabitha had used witchcraft to orchestrate the accident, but it had never been proven. It was all dismissed as small-town gossip.

Claudette felt a chill crawl up her spine. Was it possible? Could Tabitha have been responsible for that accident all those years ago?

And if so, could she have used the same dark magic to harm Jerrimi and her son?

The weight of the realization settled heavily in Claudette's chest. She stared at the screen, piecing together what she knew: Jerrimi had found something while packing. Something that had made him want to confront Tabitha. But he never got the chance—he and their son had died before they could talk. And now, it seemed that accident might not have been an accident at all.

Claudette's mind raced, her heart pounding with the weight of this discovery. If Tabitha was willing to kill her husband and son to keep her secrets hidden, what else was she capable of?

She grabbed her phone, her hands trembling as she dialed Brian's number. It rang once, twice, and then he answered.

"Claudette? What's going on?"

"Brian," she said, her voice low and urgent. "I found something—something about Tabitha. I don't think Jerrimi and his son's accident was an accident. I think she killed them."

There was a long silence on the other end of the line.

"What are you talking about?" Brian finally asked his voice tight with disbelief.

"She was into witchcraft," Claudette explained quickly, her words tumbling out in a rush. "Back in high school, she was obsessed with this football player. When he dumped her, there was an accident—he and his girlfriend died on the way to prom. People said it was an accident, but there were rumors that Tabitha was involved. That she used magic to cause it."

"Are you serious?" Brian sounded both shocked and horrified.

"I didn't want to believe it either, but there's more," Claudette continued, her voice shaking. "Jerrimi—Tabitha's husband; I thought Morghan said she recently lost her son and husband. The article is dated back four years ago. Why would she lie about that? It also said that he had informed Tabitha on their last phone call together that he needed to talk to her. But before they could, he and their son died in a car crash. Brian, I think she did something to them. I think she used magic to kill them."

Brian's breath hitched on the other end. "You think she murdered her own family?"

"Yes," Claudette said firmly. "And I think she's using the same kind of magic on Morghan. That scarf it's part of it. We need to figure out what's going on before it's too late."

Brian was silent for a moment, processing the enormity of what Claudette was saying.

"What do we do?" he finally asked, his voice filled with both fear and determination.

"We need help," Claudette said. "This is beyond us. We're not just dealing with a crazy person—we're dealing with someone who's using dark magic. I've heard of people who specialize in breaking curses, in dealing with this kind of thing. We need to find someone who can help us fight back."

Brian exhaled sharply. "Okay. Find someone. I'll stay with Morghan, but we need to move fast. If what you're saying is true, we can't afford to wait."

Claudette nodded, though he couldn't see her. "I'll handle it. Just be careful, Brian. Don't let Tabitha anywhere near you or Morghan."

"I won't," Brian promised, his voice resolute.

They hung up, and Claudette's mind whirled with the weight of her discovery. Tabitha wasn't just a grieving widow or a scorned woman—she was a predator, someone who had been using witchcraft for years to manipulate and destroy anyone who got in her way.

Claudette knew they were up against something dangerous, something far more powerful than they had imagined.

But she wasn't going to let Tabitha win. Not this time.

With a deep breath, Claudette began searching for someone who could help them. Someone who knew how to fight back against the kind of darkness Tabitha had unleashed.

Time was running out, but they still had a chance.

And Claudette wasn't going to let her friend be the next victim.

Chapter Nineteen
A Friends Wrath

Claudette kissed her twins gently on their foreheads, trying to ignore the weight pressing down on her chest as she pulled away. Her husband, Corey, stood by the doorway, holding one of their daughters' hands, his face creased with concern.

"Are you sure about this?" Corey asked quietly, his voice thick with worry. "You're going out there to find someone we don't even know... and dealing with something we don't fully understand."

Claudette straightened her sweater, her resolve solid. "I don't have a choice, Corey. Morghan's life is at stake, and Brian... he's in over his head. This woman I found she's supposed to be an expert in dealing with dark magic. If anyone can help us, it's her."

Corey's brow lifted. "Just be careful. I don't want you getting wrapped up in something you can't handle. What about the twins? They're worried about you."

Claudette knelt down, brushing a hand through her daughter's hair. "I'll be back soon, sweeties. Mommy just has to help Auntie Morghan. You know how brave she is, right? Just like you two."

Her daughters nodded, but their eyes were wide, sensing the gravity of the situation. She gave Corey a slight smile before slipping out the door. As she stepped into the cool evening air, her heart hammered in her chest. There was no room for hesitation now; Morghan was running out of time, and she needed to find help before Tabitha made her final move.

Claudette had spent the last several hours researching and making phone calls until she finally found someone who could help, a woman named Reina. According to the few references Claudette had tracked down, Reina was a spiritual practitioner who specialized in undoing dark magic. She was the best hope they had.

She reached her car, taking a deep breath to steady herself as she drove toward Reina's small, isolated cottage on the outskirts of town. With each passing mile, her mind swirled with thoughts of Tabitha, Brian, and, most of all, Morghan. They were in real danger. She couldn't fail them now.

Meanwhile, back at Brian and Morghan's house, Brian sat by Morghan's bedside, watching her with a mixture of love and fear. She looked fragile, her skin pale and clammy, her breathing shallow. Every now and then, she would stir, her body wracked with a coughing fit that left her gasping for air.

"Brian," Morghan whispered, her voice barely audible, "what's happening to me?"

Brian squeezed her hand gently, trying to keep his emotions in check. "You're going to be okay, babe. I promise. Claudette's working on something, and we're going to figure this out."

But deep down, Brian wasn't so sure. Morghan's condition had only worsened over the past few days, and despite the doctors' best efforts, they couldn't figure out what was wrong. It wasn't the flu; it wasn't a simple allergic reaction. Whatever this was, it had a dark grip on her—and Brian was terrified that they were running out of time to save her.

The doorbell rang, and Brian's stomach twisted. He wasn't expecting anyone. His heart raced as he hurried downstairs to answer the door, his mind immediately thinking of Tabitha. He opened the door, and there she was, standing on his front porch with that familiar, disarming smile.

"Brian," Tabitha said softly, her voice dripping with false concern. "I heard about Morghan's condition. I just wanted to stop by and see if there's anything I can do to help."

Brian's blood ran cold. He didn't trust her—he hadn't since the incident at the Soup Bar. But he couldn't just turn her away without raising suspicion. He needed to play it smart.

"She's resting right now," Brian said, keeping his voice steady. "We've got everything under control."

Tabitha tilted her head slightly, her eyes scanning his face as if she were searching for some sign of weakness. "I understand," she said, stepping forward a little. "But if you ever need anything, I'm here for you. I know what it's like to feel powerless when someone you love is suffering."

Brian clenched his jaw, forcing a tight smile. "Thanks, Tabitha. I appreciate it, but we're handling things."

Tabitha's gaze lingered on him for a moment longer than necessary, and Brian felt a chill creep up his spine. She wasn't here out of concern—he could feel that much. This was about control. Tabitha was trying to get closer to him, to wedge herself further into their lives. And after what Claudette had uncovered, Brian couldn't afford to let that happen.

"I'll be going, then," Tabitha said with a small smile. "But don't hesitate to reach out. Sometimes... we need help from unexpected places."

As she turned to leave, Brian watched her go, his hands shaking with the effort it took to keep his anger at bay. She was playing a dangerous game, and they were all caught in the middle of it. The question was, how far was she willing to go?

Several miles away, Claudette finally arrived at the edge of a dense area where Reina's office was located. The sun was setting low in the sky; it would be dark before long. Claudette's heart pounded as she parked the car and made her way toward the small, weathered office building nestled deep in a wooded area outside of Frisco.

The air was heavy with an ancient energy, and as Claudette approached, she felt a strange sense of being watched, as if the trees themselves were alive with unseen forces. She steeled herself, knowing that this was the only chance she had to save Morghan.

She knocked on the old wooden door, and after a few moments, it creaked open. A woman in her late fifties with deep-set eyes and silver-streaked hair stood in the doorway, her presence commanding yet calm.

"You must be Claudette," Reina said, her voice rich and soothing. "I've been expecting you."

Claudette nodded, feeling the weight of her mission settling even heavier on her shoulders. "I need your help," she said, her voice trembling with urgency. "There's a woman— Tabitha—who's been using witchcraft to hurt my friend. She's made her sick, and I think she's done something much worse in the past."

Reina stepped aside, motioning for Claudette to enter. "Come in. We have much to discuss."

Inside, the air was thick with the scent of herbs and incense, and the walls were lined with shelves of jars and old books. It felt like stepping into another world, one where the veil between the natural and the supernatural was thin.

Reina gestured for Claudette to sit at a small wooden table, her eyes studying her carefully. "This Tabitha... her magic is old. Tainted. She comes from a long line of practitioners, and the darkness she wields is not easily undone."

Claudette's heart sank. "Is there anything we can do?"

Reina nodded slowly, her expression grave. "There are ways to break her hold. But it won't be easy. The scarf you mentioned—it's an object of power. She's using it to siphon energy from your friend, to weaken her. We'll need to destroy it, but not before severing its connection to the spell."

Claudette leaned forward, her mind racing. "How do we do that?"

Reina placed her hands on the table, her fingers lightly tracing symbols into the wood. "We'll need to perform a counter-ritual. It will take time and preparation. I will need the scarf, and I'll need to know everything about Tabitha—her history, her connections, everything you can give me."

Claudette nodded, relief flooding her. "I'll get you whatever you need. Just please... help us stop her."

Reina's gaze softened. "We will stop her, but you must be prepared. She won't let go easily, and there will be consequences."

Claudette's stomach churned, but she nodded. "I'm ready. Whatever it takes."

Reina stood, moving toward a shelf lined with vials of herbs and oils. "Then let's begin. Time is running out."

As Claudette watched Reina gather the materials for the ritual, her mind flashed to Morghan, weak and bedridden, and to Brian, fighting to protect the woman he loved from an enemy he couldn't fully understand.

Chapter Twenty
Confronted

Claudette's mind swirled as she drove away from Reina's office, her thoughts racing with what the spiritual practitioner had told her. Reina's instructions had been clear: the scarf was the key to breaking the dark spell that Tabitha had cast over Morghan. Without it, they were powerless to counter the magic slowly draining the life from her.

But retrieving the scarf was easier said than done.

Claudette wondered if the scarf was at her home, hoping she had misplaced it or that Tabitha hadn't truly taken it. But deep down, she knew the truth. Tabitha had the scarf. It was why Morghan had grown so sick, why nothing the doctors did was working. The scarf was infused with Tabitha's darkness, and the only way to sever its connection to Morghan was to get it back.

Now, Claudette was left with one option: she had to confront Tabitha.

Her stomach churned at the thought, but there was no turning back. She had tried reaching out to Brian and Erich earlier to warn them, but the calls had gone straight to voicemail. They were likely at the hospital with Morghan. She was on her own now, and the clock was ticking.

As the city lights blurred past her, Claudette's phone buzzed on the passenger seat. She glanced at it, another missed call from Corey. She hadn't told him everything, just enough to keep him and the kids safe. But now, as she approached Tabitha's street, the weight of what she was about to do pressed on her like a lead weight.

Claudette pulled up a few houses away from Tabitha's. The dark outline of Tabitha's home loomed in the distance, its windows dimly lit by the faint glow of a single lamp. Claudette had hoped that she might catch Tabitha out or find the house empty, but there was no such luck tonight. The eerie stillness of the street sent a chill down her spine.

She shut off her car, taking a deep breath to steady her nerves. Her fingers curled around the strap of her bag, where she kept a small vial of protective herbs that Reina had given her. It wasn't much, but it gave her a sense of security. Claudette didn't fully understand magic, but she had seen enough strange things lately to know that she was walking into dangerous territory.

Claudette approached the house cautiously, her heart racing in her chest. As she made her way up the narrow path leading to the front door, she could feel the oppressive energy radiating from the house, like an invisible force pushing against her.

She knocked lightly, hoping that maybe, just maybe, Tabitha wouldn't be home. But as the door creaked open, Claudette's heart sped up.

Tabitha stood in the doorway, her eyes sharp and watchful, a smile curling at the corners of her lips. She looked almost serene, her dark hair cascading over her shoulders, but Claudette could feel the menace behind her calm demeanor.

"Claudette," Tabitha said smoothly, her voice dripping with fakeness. "What a surprise. What brings you here?"

Claudette swallowed hard, trying to keep her voice steady. "I need to talk to you. About Morghan."

Tabitha's smile didn't falter, but her eyes darkened. "Morghan? What's wrong with her?"

"You know what's wrong with her," Claudette said, her voice low and firm. "She's sick, Tabitha. And I know you're behind it."

Tabitha's eyes narrowed, her smile slipping just slightly. "I don't know what you're talking about. Morghan's been ill for days. I've been nothing but concerned for her."

Claudette stepped forward, her jaw clenched. "You took something from her house. A scarf. I need it back."

There was a long, tense silence as Tabitha studied Claudette, her gaze cold and calculating. Then, she tilted her head slightly, her voice soft and condescending. "You think a scarf is going to help Morghan? How quaint."

Claudette's hands balled into fists at her sides. "I don't care what you think. Give me the scarf, and this will all end."

Tabitha's smile grew wider, more sinister. "You think you're in control here, Claudette? You don't understand what you're dealing with. This is far beyond you."

Claudette's heart pounded in her chest, but she refused to back down. She could feel the protective herbs pressing against her thigh through her bag, reminding her of Reina's words: *You must retrieve the scarf, no matter what.*

"I'm not afraid of you," Claudette said, her voice shaking with both fear and determination. "You're going to give me that scarf, and you're going to stop hurting Morghan."

Tabitha let out a soft, amused chuckle, taking a step forward until she was just inches away from Claudette. "Afraid? No, you're not afraid yet. But you will be."

Before Claudette could react, Tabitha's hand shot out, grabbing her wrist with a grip like iron. A cold shock ran through Claudette's body, and she gasped, trying to pull away. But Tabitha's grip tightened, her eyes locking onto Claudette's with an intensity that sent a chill through her soul.

"You're meddling in things you don't understand," Tabitha whispered, her voice filled with dark promise. "Morghan's fate is sealed. There's nothing you—or anyone—can do to change that."

With a sudden surge of strength, Claudette yanked her arm free, stumbling back a few steps, her heart racing. Tabitha stood there, calm and unbothered, as if nothing had happened.

"You should leave now," Tabitha said softly, her voice dripping with menace. "Before you get hurt."

Claudette's breath came in short, ragged bursts as she took another step back, her mind screaming at her to leave. But she couldn't—she couldn't just walk away.

"I'll be back," Claudette said, her voice trembling but firm. "And when I do, You will be stopped!"

Tabitha's smile widened. "I'll be waiting."

Without another word, Claudette turned and fled, her legs shaky as she hurried back to her car. Her heart pounded in her ears, and her hands trembled as she fumbled for the keys, the cold grip of fear still lingering on her skin.

She had failed. She hadn't retrieved the scarf, and now Tabitha knew that Claudette was onto her. The situation was worse than she thought.

But as Claudette sped away, her mind whirled with determination. Tabitha had the upper hand for now, but she wasn't going to stop. Morghan's life depended on it.

She needed to get back to Reina, and fast.

Whatever it took, Claudette would find a way to break the dark hold Tabitha had over Morghan. Time was running out, but she wasn't giving up. Not yet!

Chapter Twenty-One
Followed by Darkness

Erich gripped the steering wheel tighter as he sped toward Brian and Morghan's house, Claudette's voice still ringing in his ears from their earlier phone call. It was hard to wrap his head around everything she had told him. Witchcraft? Dark rituals? It all sounded like something out of a horror movie, but he had seen enough strange behavior from Tabitha to know something wasn't right. And now, with Morghan's condition worsening, they couldn't afford to ignore any possibility, no matter how bizarre.

As he pulled up to Brian and Morghan's house, Erich noticed Brian standing outside on the porch, pacing back and forth. He looked exhausted, dark circles under his eyes, his movements jittery with worry.

Erich parked the car and jogged up the steps. "Brian, what's going on? How's Morghan?"

Brian looked up, his face a mixture of fear and frustration. "It's bad, Erich. She's not getting any better, and the doctors can't figure out what's wrong with her. I don't know how much longer she can hold on like this."

Erich swallowed hard, nodding. "Claudette told me what she found out about Tabitha. I know it sounds insane, but if she's really behind this, we need to take it seriously. Maybe we should get Morghan back to the hospital. She needs medical help, but if it's something... supernatural, we need Claudette's friend to act fast."

Brian sighed, rubbing his temples. "I've been thinking the same thing. I'm just scared that every time we take her to the hospital, she gets worse. But we don't have a choice anymore. Let's get her there, and I'll call Claudette when we're on the way. She said she's working with someone who can help, but I don't know how long it'll take."

Erich clapped Brian on the shoulder, offering some reassurance. "We'll figure this out. Let's get Morghan to the hospital, and we'll go from there."

Together, the two men rushed inside and helped Morghan get dressed. She was weak, so much weaker than even the day before. Her skin had grown paler, her eyes sunken, and she struggled to stand as Brian wrapped his arms around her for support.

"I'm so tired," Morghan whispered, her voice barely audible. "I don't know if I can make it to the hospital."

"You can," Brian said softly, his voice filled with both love and fear. "We'll get you there. Just hold on."

With Erich's help, they carefully loaded her into the car, trying not to show their panic as they buckled her in. Brian climbed into the driver's seat while Erich took the passenger side, glancing back at Morghan every few seconds, his heart heavy with worry.

As they pulled away from the house, none of them noticed the dark car parked just a few houses down. Tabitha sat inside, her eyes glued to Brian's vehicle, her fingers tapping lightly on the steering wheel as a small, satisfied smile curled at the corners of her lips.

They were taking Morghan to the hospital again, perfect.

Tabitha had been waiting for this opportunity. And with Claudette in the way now, it was time to get this over with. She needed to get her man once and for all. She knew Morghan was growing weaker by the day, the spell working exactly as intended, but it wasn't enough. Morghan was still alive, still clinging to her pathetic existence. Tabitha needed to finish the job, and now that they were headed to the hospital, she saw her chance.

She waited for Brian's car to pull out of sight before she started her engine and followed at a distance, careful not to be noticed. Her heart raced with anticipation. She had been patient long enough, and tonight, she would be rid of Morghan for good.

At the hospital, Brian and Erich helped Morghan out of the car, rushing her into the emergency room. Brian's heart was pounding in his chest as he spoke to the triage nurse, trying to explain the situation while fighting back the rising panic that threatened to overwhelm him.

"She's been sick for days," Brian said, his voice shaking. "We don't know what's causing it. She's barely able to breathe on her own. Please, she needs help."

The nurse nodded, quickly calling for a doctor and a gurney to be brought over. Within minutes, Morghan was being wheeled into a private room, and Brian and Erich were ushered into the waiting area to fill out paperwork.

Brian's hands trembled as he signed the forms, his eyes darting between the nurse and the hallway where Morghan had disappeared. Erich stayed close by, trying to offer some calm amid the storm.

"She's in good hands, Brian," Erich said quietly. "We'll get through this."

But neither of them noticed the shadow that slipped past the front desk, unnoticed in the chaos of the busy ER. Tabitha walked calmly down the hall, her expression unreadable as she made her way toward Morghan's room. She had timed it perfectly. Brian was distracted, and the hospital staff were too busy to pay attention to the woman who appeared to be just another visitor.

Tabitha felt the familiar pull of magic coursing through her veins, her connection to the spell growing stronger as she approached the room. She knew Morghan was weak, hanging by a thread. All it would take was one final push, one last touch, to sever the life from her body.

As she reached the door to Morghan's room, she paused, glancing around to make sure no one was watching. The hallway was empty, and the sound of nurses and doctors rushing through the ER was distant, muffled.

Tabitha's fingers curled around the door handle, her smile returning as she prepared to enter the room.

But before she could open the door, a voice behind her froze her in place.

"Can I help you?"

Tabitha turned slowly, her face an unreadable mask of innocence. A young nurse stood a few feet away, her expression polite but questioning.

"I was just coming to check on a friend," Tabitha said smoothly, her voice dripping with false sincerity. "She's very sick."

The nurse glanced at the door and then back at Tabitha. "I'm sorry, but visiting hours are over, and we need to keep the area clear for now. You'll have to wait in the waiting room until the doctors give the okay."

Tabitha's smile faltered for just a moment, but she quickly recovered, nodding. "Of course. I understand."

She turned and walked back down the hall, her fists clenched at her sides. She hadn't expected interference, but it didn't matter. She would wait. Brian would eventually leave, and when he did, she would finish what she started.

Back in the waiting room, Brian and Erich sat in uneasy silence, neither of them able to shake the heavy feeling of dread that had settled over them.

But neither of them knew just how close Tabitha had come to taking Morghan from them.

And she wasn't finished yet.

Chapter Twenty-Two
A New Plan

The hum of the car engine was the only sound that filled Claudette's mind as she sped down the dark road. Her breath was still uneven, her body tense from the encounter with Tabitha. The woman's cold, knowing gaze haunted her, and the feel of her icy grip lingered on Claudette's skin, sending a chill through her every time she thought about it.

She had failed to retrieve the scarf, failed to get the one thing that Reina needed to break Tabitha's spell. But there was no time to dwell on that. Claudette knew she couldn't go back home empty-handed. She had to regroup, talk to Reina, and figure out their next move. Tabitha was dangerous, but she wasn't invincible. At least, that's what Claudette kept telling herself as she drove back to the small office hidden in the woods.

When she finally arrived, the thick scent of herbs and smoke greeted her before she even knocked on the door. Reina was already waiting, her expression calm but unreadable as she opened the door and gestured for Claudette to come inside.

"You couldn't get it," Reina said, more a statement than a question.

Claudette nodded, her voice tight with frustration. "She has it. She knows exactly what she's doing, and she's not going to give it up easily."

Reina closed the door behind her, the soft crackle of burning herbs filling the air as she moved toward the small altar set up in the corner. "Tabitha's witchcraft is strong, and she's been planning this for a long time. The scarf is only part of the ritual, but it's crucial. Without it, the bond between her and Morghan remains intact."

Claudette sank into a chair, her exhaustion weighing heavily on her shoulders. "I don't know how to get it from her, Reina. She's playing games, and I'm running out of time. Morghan's getting worse by the minute."

Reina sat across from her, her eyes soft but serious. "There are other ways to break the spell. It will be more dangerous, but it can be done. However, if you fail... the consequences will be severe."

Claudette's heart pounded in her chest. "What do I have to do?"

Reina stood and moved to a shelf filled with jars of herbs, powders, and talismans. She selected a few, laying them out carefully on the table between them. "This is a counter-ritual, one that targets the source of the magic, not just the object. It's a form of spiritual warfare, and it requires strength—both physical and mental. You will be the one to sever the connection between Tabitha and Morghan."

Claudette stared at the materials in front of her, her pulse quickening. She wasn't prepared for this. She had never done anything like it before. But if it was the only way to save Morghan, she couldn't back down now.

"What do I need to do?" she asked, her voice steadier than she felt.

Reina picked up a small pouch of herbs and handed it to her. "You'll need to draw Tabitha's energy away from Morghan. This mixture will weaken the bond, but it will also put you at risk. Tabitha's magic is old and powerful, and if she realizes what you're doing, she will retaliate."

Claudette nodded, swallowing hard. "I understand."

Reina continued, her voice low and steady. "You'll need to perform the ritual at a location that's connected to both Tabitha and Morghan. The hospital is too public, but somewhere significant, somewhere Tabitha's magic has already left a mark, would work. You'll also need something personal of Morghan's, something that connects her to the scarf."

Claudette's mind raced, thinking of the places where Morghan and Tabitha had crossed paths. Then it hit her, the BBQ! That's the day Tabitha had been at their house, surrounded by their friends, making herself a part of their lives. That was where it had all started.

"I'll do it at the house," Claudette said, her voice firm. "That's where it all began. It feels right."

Reina nodded approvingly. "Good. But remember, you must act quickly. The longer Morghan is under Tabitha's control, the more power Tabitha gains."

Claudette stood, pocketing the pouch of herbs. "I'll head there now. I'll find something of Morghan's at the house and perform the ritual tonight."

Reina placed a hand on Claudette's shoulder, her eyes filled with both warmth and warning. "Stay strong. Trust your instincts. Tabitha may be powerful, but she isn't invincible."

Claudette nodded, her heart pounding as she left the office and headed back to her car. The weight of what lay ahead pressed down on her, but there was no time to dwell on the fear.

She had a plan now.

Back at the hospital, Brian sat in a stiff waiting room chair, his eyes red-rimmed from lack of sleep. He had been by Morghan's side for hours, watching helplessly as her condition continued to deteriorate. The doctors were doing everything they could, but nothing seemed to work. Morghan was slipping away, and Brian's heart was breaking with every shallow breath she took.

Erich sat beside him, his expression grim. "She's strong, Brian. She's going to pull through."

Brian shook his head, his hands trembling. "I don't know, man. Nothing's working. I don't know how much longer she can fight this."

Erich placed a reassuring hand on Brian's shoulder, but even he didn't have any words left. They were both running on fumes, waiting for Claudette's call, hoping that whatever help she was getting from Reina would be enough.

Then, Brian's phone buzzed. He grabbed it immediately, hoping it was Claudette with some news. But when he looked at the screen, his stomach dropped.

It wasn't Claudette.

It was Tabitha.

He stared at the phone, his pulse speeding up. "Why is she calling me?" he muttered, more to himself than to Erich.

Erich frowned. "What do you mean?"

"Tabitha," Brian said, showing him the phone. "She's calling."

Erich's eyes darkened with suspicion. "Don't answer it."

Brian nodded, his fingers hovering over the screen. He ignored the call, but the moment it stopped, a text popped up.

"I'm here if you need me. I can help."

A chill ran down Brian's spine as he looked around the waiting room, suddenly feeling as if someone was watching them. He stood abruptly, his body tense. "She's here. I know she's here."

Erich stood, his voice sharp. "Brian, we need to get back to Morghan's room. Now."

They rushed down the hallway, their footsteps echoing in the sterile corridor. Brian's heart raced as they neared Morghan's room, the feeling of dread tightening around him like a noose.

When they entered, Morghan was still lying there, weak and barely conscious, but the room was eerily quiet.

Too quiet.

Chapter Twenty-Three
A Voice of Reason

Claudette's heart raced as she sped through the dark streets, the dim headlights barely cutting through the fog that had begun to settle over the town. Her fingers gripped the steering wheel tightly, with tension, as she thought about the ritual she was about to perform. This wasn't something she had ever imagined herself doing, but there was no turning back now. Morghan's life depended on it, and time was running out.

The pouch of herbs Reina had given her sat on the passenger seat, the scent of sage and jasmine filling the small space of the car. Claudette had gone over the instructions in her head a dozen times. She knew exactly what she needed to do, but the weight of what was at stake pressed down on her like a heavy blanket.

She had to stay focused.

As Brian and Morghan's house came into view, Claudette reached for her phone. She had to let Erich and Brian know what she was about to do. They needed to be prepared for the ritual, for the danger that came with confronting Tabitha's witchcraft.

The phone rang twice before Erich's voice came through on the other end.

"Claudette?" His voice was strained, filled with both concern and relief. "Where are you?"

"I'm on my way to the house," Claudette said, trying to keep her voice steady. "I have what I need for the ritual, but things didn't go as planned. I couldn't get the scarf from Tabitha, so I have to do this without it. Reina gave me a counter-ritual. It's risky, but it's our only option."

There was a pause on the other end of the line, and Claudette could hear Erich's breath quicken. "You're doing the ritual now? At the house?"

"Yes," Claudette replied. "The house is connected to both Morghan and Tabitha; that's where the scarf went missing. It's the best place to break the bond between them. I have the garage code to let myself in."

Erich cursed under his breath. "Brian's still here at the hospital with Morghan. She's getting worse, Claudette. I don't know how much longer she can hold on."

"I know," Claudette said softly, the weight of his words heavy on her chest. "That's why I'm doing this now. If I can break the connection, it will weaken the spell and give Morghan a chance to recover."

Another pause, this time longer, before Erich's voice came through, more determined now. "What do you need us to do?"

"I need you to keep Brian with Morghan," Claudette instructed. "Don't let him leave the hospital.

"Tabitha's close; we believe she may have been here at the hospital earlier. I don't know if she's still here, but I won't let Brian leave Morghan's side."

"If the ritual works, she'll feel the effects immediately. But if Tabitha realizes what I'm doing, she could try to stop me."

Erich exhaled sharply. "Okay. I'll keep him here. But be careful, Claudette. This woman... she's dangerous."

"I know," Claudette said, her voice firm. "But I'm not letting her win. I won't let Morghan die because of her."

Erich's voice softened, a hint of gratitude breaking through his concern. "Thank you, Claudette. For doing this. I don't know what we'd do without you."

Claudette swallowed the lump in her throat, forcing herself to stay focused. "We're not losing Morghan, Erich. Not on my watch."

Claudette ended the call with Erich and proceeded to get out of the car. As she stepped out of the car, her phone rang again. Brian's name appeared on the screen.

"Brian?" she said, trying to keep her voice steady despite the rush of adrenaline coursing through her veins. "I'm heading to your place now. I've got everything I need to perform the ritual. We can stop this, Brian; I just need a few hours."

There was a pause on the other end of the line, the silence stretching uncomfortably long. When Brian finally spoke, his voice was strained but firm.

"Claudette, stop."

"Erich just told me everything, and we're not doing this." Her heart skipped a beat. "What do you mean, stop? I'm almost there, Brian. I can break the spell. I talked to Reina, and she…"

"I don't care what Reina said," Brian interrupted, his voice sharper now. "Enough with all this witchcraft, Claudette. I can't do it anymore. I just want it to stop."

Claudette blinked, stopping in her footsteps approaching the front of their home. as she processed his words. "Brian, listen to me. This isn't about belief, and it's real. Tabitha's done something to Morghan, and if I don't act now, it might be too late."

Brian sighed, the exhaustion clear in his voice. "I know you mean well, but Morghan's at the hospital, and the doctors are finally making progress. She's stabilizing, Claudette. They think she's going to pull through. I don't want to complicate things with all this... magic stuff."

"Brian, it's not just about the doctors!" Claudette's voice rose, frustration bubbling up inside her. "The doctors don't know what's really going on. You said to yourself they couldn't explain why she got sick in the first place. This isn't just some medical mystery, and it's Tabitha."

There was another long pause, and Claudette could hear Brian's breathing on the other end of the line. When he spoke again, his tone was softer, almost pleading.

"Claudette, I love Morghan more than anything, and I can't stand the thought of losing her. But right now, I just want to trust that the hospital is the best place for her. I don't want any more rituals or magic, no more guessing. Just come to the hospital. Please."

Claudette's heart sank. She had never heard Brian sound so defeated. She knew how hard this was for him, watching Morghan suffer, feeling powerless to stop it. But the thought of abandoning the ritual, of not doing everything she could to break Tabitha's hold on Morghan, made her stomach twist.

"Brian, if I come to the hospital, there's nothing more I can do," she said quietly. "The ritual is the only way to stop Tabitha truly. What if she comes after you next? What if Morghan's recovery is just a temporary fix?"

"I don't care about Tabitha," Brian replied, his voice hardening. "I care about Morghan, and right now, she's getting better. That's all I want. Please, Claudette, just come here. I need you here, not chasing after this witchcraft stuff."

Claudette bit her lip, her eyes darting between the house and the phone in her hand. She had never been one to back down from a fight, especially when it involved the people she loved. But this wasn't her decision to make; it was Brian's. And if he was asking her to stand down, how could she refuse?

She let out a long breath, her heart heavy with indecision. "Are you sure?" she asked, her voice softer now.

"Yes," Brian said, his tone resolute. "Come to the hospital, Claudette. Morghan needs you here. I need you here."

Claudette's hands trembled as she held onto the phone, her mind spinning with conflicting thoughts. She had prepared for this for the ritual, for facing down Tabitha's dark magic. But Brian's words had shaken something inside her. Maybe, just maybe, he was right. Maybe they didn't need more witchcraft. Maybe all they needed was to trust that things were finally turning around.

"Okay," she whispered, the decision sinking in slowly. "I'm coming to the hospital."

"Thank you," Brian replied, relief washing over his voice. "Drive safe, and I'll see you soon."

They hung up, and Claudette walked back to her vehicle. She sat in the car for a moment, her hands resting on the steering wheel. The path she had been so certain of moments ago now felt clouded, uncertain. But she knew one thing, Brian needed her, and Morghan was beginning to recover. Maybe that was enough for now.

With a heavy heart, Claudette pressed the ignition button and headed toward the hospital. As she drove, the quiet weight of what she had left behind the ritual, the confrontation with Tabitha—pressed down on her like a shadow. She wasn't sure if this was the right decision, but for now, she had chosen the only path that mattered.

She was going to be with her friends. They would face whatever came next together.

As the hospital's lights came into view, Claudette's phone buzzed again. This time, it wasn't Brian.

It was a message from Reina: "I felt the energy shift. Be careful, Claudette. The darkness isn't gone."

Claudette swallowed hard as she read the message. She didn't know what that meant, but for now, she pushed it to the back of her mind.

For now, she was heading to the hospital, and they would deal with the rest, whatever that was when it came.

Chapter Twenty-Four
A Call to Faith

Brian stood in the quiet hospital hallway after ending the call with Claudette, leaning against the wall outside of Morghan's room. The hum of the fluorescent lights above barely registered in his mind as he stared down at his phone. Morghan was resting peacefully now, but the weight of the past few days was pressing down on him like a heavy fog. The doctors had said she was improving, but deep down, Brian knew something else had been at play. Something darker.

His thoughts drifted to Tabitha, her obsession, the manipulation, and Morghan's accident. He didn't want to believe in the power of her witchcraft, but he couldn't deny the effect it had on Morghan. Yet now, standing here, watching his wife slowly recover, Brian felt something stirring inside him—a quiet voice reminding him of what truly mattered.

He scrolled through his contacts, his thumb hovering over his mother's name. Morghan's parents were on the way into town, but he hadn't called her yet; he hadn't wanted to worry her with all that had happened. But now, more than ever, he needed to hear her voice. He needed her strength.

With a deep breath, he hit the call button and held the phone to his ear. The line rang only twice before she answered, her voice filled with warmth and concern.

"Brian? Hey, Is everything okay, sweetheart?"

Brian swallowed hard, his voice catching in his throat. "Mom... it's Morghan. She's been really sick. We almost lost her."

There was a brief pause on the other end, and when his mother spoke again, her voice was soft but steady. "Tell me everything, Brian. I'm listening."

Brian exhaled slowly, his words tumbling out in a rush as he explained the past few days—the sudden illness, the hospital stays, the doctors who couldn't explain what was happening, and Tabitha's involvement. He told her about Claudette, the ritual she had planned, and how it had all spiraled into something beyond his control.

By the time he finished, his chest felt tight, and his hands were shaking. For the first time in days, he allowed himself to feel the fear that had been gnawing at him fully.

"Mom, I don't know what to do," he admitted, his voice cracking. "I don't want to believe in all this witchcraft stuff, but I can't ignore what's been happening. And now, Claudette thinks the only way to fix it is with some ritual. But... I don't know if that's the answer."

His mother was silent for a moment, letting his words sink in. Then, with the calm assurance that only a mother could provide, she spoke.

"Brian, you know that witchcraft and dark magic have no power over the love you and Morghan share. They might try to confuse or mislead you, but at the end of the day, there is only one true source of power. And that power comes from God."

Brian closed his eyes, leaning back against the wall as his mother's words washed over him. He had grown up with faith, and it had always been an important part of his life. But in the chaos of the past few days, he had forgotten the most important thing—his belief in something greater than all of this.

"I'm not saying that what's happened isn't real," his mother continued. "But you and Morghan have something much stronger than any darkness Tabitha could ever bring. You have love, and you have faith. And if you want to protect Morghan, then you need to lean on both."

Brian felt a lump rise in his throat. "What do I do, Mom?"

"You pray," she said simply. "You pray for her healing, for her protection, and for strength to see this through. And you believe, Brian. You believe that God is watching over her. No matter what's happening around you, no matter what Tabitha has tried to do, God's love is more powerful than any spell or curse. You need to put your trust in Him."

Brian swallowed hard, the weight of his mother's words settling into his heart. He had been so focused on the fear, on the uncertainty, that he had forgotten the one thing that had always guided him—his faith.

"You're right," Brian whispered, his voice thick with emotion. "I need to pray. I need to trust that God will heal her."

His mother's voice softened, filled with love. "I'll pray with you, Brian. Right now."

Brian closed his eyes, bowing his head as his mother began to pray, her words gentle but strong. She prayed for Morghan's healing, for protection from any darkness, and for the power of God's love to surround them both. Brian's heart swelled with emotion as he whispered his own prayers, tears sliding down his cheeks as he released the fear that had held him captive.

As they finished the prayer, Brian felt a deep sense of peace settle over him. For the first time in days, he felt calm. He felt hope.

"Thank you, Mom," he said quietly, wiping his tears away. "I needed that."

"You're going to get through this, Brian," she replied, her voice warm. "God's already working. You just have to trust Him."

They said their goodbyes, and as Brian hung up, he felt a renewed sense of purpose. He wasn't going to rely on rituals or magic to save Morghan. He was going to trust in God's love—and in his own love for his wife.

Chapter Twenty-Five
Unbreakable Bond

With a deep breath, Brian stepped back into Morghan's room, his heart steady as he approached her bedside. She was still resting, her chest rising and falling in slow, even breaths. The machines around her beeped softly, but Brian's focus was entirely on her.

He sat down beside her, taking her hand in his, and for the first time in days, he wasn't afraid.

"Morghan," he whispered, his voice full of love. "I know you can hear me. I love you so much, and I know you're going to get through this. God's watching over you, and I'm right here with you. We're going to be okay."

He bowed his head and prayed again, this time feeling the strength of his love for her guiding his words. He prayed for her healing, for her protection, and for the power of God's love to bring them through this darkness.

As he sat there, praying, Brian felt something shift—something intangible but real. The air in the room seemed lighter, and a sense of peace filled the space.

Erich fought back tears as he witnessed the heartfelt prayer Brian had just prayed over his wife.

"I'm going to grab a coffee," Erich said softly, breaking the silence. "You want anything?"

Brian shook his head, his voice barely a whisper. "No, I'm good. Thanks, man."

Erich gave a quick nod and stepped out of the room, leaving Brian alone with Morghan.

As soon as the door clicked shut, Brian exhaled a shaky breath and leaned forward, resting his forehead gently on Morghan's hand. His eyes burned with unshed tears as the knot of fear that had consumed him felt lighter.

"Morghan..." he whispered. His fingers traced the outline of her hand, the familiar softness of her skin grounding him in the moment. He stared at her peaceful face, so different from the vibrant woman he had loved for years.

"I've been thinking about the first time we met," Brian continued, his voice soft and full of emotion. "Back at that high school football game. You were wearing that old letterman jacket that didn't even belong to you—it was your brother's. I thought you were the coolest girl I'd ever seen. And even though we didn't start dating until college, I knew, even then, that you were the one for me."

Brian's lips curved into a small, sad smile as he recalled those memories. He closed his eyes for a moment, letting the nostalgia wash over him like a balm against the pain.

"You were so different back then," he said with a quiet chuckle. "Confident, bold. You weren't afraid to tell me when I was being an idiot. Remember that time I almost dropped out of school to work for my uncle's landscaping business? You talked me out of it in five minutes flat."

He paused, swallowing back the lump in his throat. "We've had so many good times, Morghan. Even before Amiya came along, it was always you and me against the world. I think about that road trip we took across the country, just the two of us, stopping at every random little town along the way. We didn't have a care in the world. I loved every minute of it because I was with you."

Brian's voice cracked as he spoke, his emotions bubbling up to the surface. "You're my everything. You've always been my everything. And I can't lose you. Not now, not ever. I don't care what the doctors say—I know you're still in there, fighting. You're the strongest person I've ever known, and I need you to keep fighting."

His grip on her hand tightened as if holding her would tether her to him and keep her from slipping away. The sound of the machines faded into the background as Brian poured his heart out, his love for her radiating through the room.

"I remember the day you told me you were pregnant with Amiya," Brian said, his voice thick with emotion. "I couldn't believe it. I was so scared, but you... you were ready. You were so sure of everything like you always are. You've always been the one holding us together, keeping me grounded. I don't know how to be without you, Morghan."

He leaned closer, his voice a whisper. "Please don't leave me. I love you. I love you more than anything in this world."

As Brian spoke, the door to the room stood slightly ajar, unnoticed by him. Just outside, in the dimly lit hallway, stood Tabitha. She had followed Brian and Erich to the hospital, determined to finish what she had started. She had planned to wait for the perfect moment to enter the room and ensure that Morghan wouldn't recover.

But now, standing there, listening to Brian's words, something unexpected stirred within her.

His voice, filled with raw emotion and love, cut through the fog of anger and jealousy that had driven her for so long. The devotion he had for Morghan, the woman she had been trying to destroy, was stronger than anything Tabitha had imagined. It was a love so deep, so pure, that it shook something inside her.

Tabitha pressed her hand to her chest, a wave of guilt crashing over her. She hadn't planned on feeling anything. She had convinced herself that getting rid of Morghan would solve all her problems—that Brian would be hers, that she could fill the emptiness inside her.

But listening to him now, she realized how wrong she had been.

Brian's love for Morghan was unbreakable. It was a bond forged through years of shared memories, challenges, and joy—things that Tabitha could never replace. Her jealousy, her need to control, had clouded her judgment, and now, for the first time, she was beginning to see the truth.

She had been using witchcraft to manipulate him, to try and tear apart something that wasn't hers to destroy. And for what? To fill a void left by the loss of her own husband and son. But no amount of manipulation or power would ever give her what Brian and Morghan shared.

Tabitha's hand hovered over the door, her fingers trembling. The familiar pull of the spell still whispered in her mind, urging her to go through with it—to finish Morghan off and take Brian for herself.

But as she listened to Brian's heartfelt words, a pang of regret pierced through her.

What have I done?

She turned away from the door, her heart racing as the weight of her actions sank in. Morghan didn't deserve this. Neither did Brian. For the first time in months, Tabitha questioned everything she had been doing—the witchcraft, the lies, the obsession.

She took a step back to get out of the hallway, her mind spinning.

Maybe it wasn't too late to stop.

Maybe she didn't have to go through with it.

But deep inside, Tabitha knew that undoing what she had started wouldn't be easy. The darkness she had embraced had its claws in her, and she wasn't sure if she could let it go.

With one last glance at the hospital room, Tabitha turned and walked away, her mind filled with the haunting realization that she had once again gone too far.

And for the first time, she didn't know if she could ever make things right.

Chapter Twenty-Six
The Weight of Consequences

She had overheard Brian's words to Morghan, the raw love he felt for his wife piercing through the fog of darkness that had consumed her for so long. As she walked through the cold hospital halls, a sense of dread settled in her stomach. She had gone too far. The witchcraft she had used to weaken Morghan, the cilantro she had slipped into her drink, it was all unraveling.

Tabitha's breath came in short, uneven bursts as she hurried through the hospital corridors, her footsteps echoing behind her. The moment she stepped outside, the cold night air hit her, snapping her out of the fog she'd been in. She made her way to the parking lot, her mind spinning with fragments of everything that had happened, everything she had done.

Once she reached her car, Tabitha fumbled with the keys, her hands trembling. She slid into the driver's seat and slammed the door shut behind her, the sound loud in the empty parking lot. She sat there, staring blankly at the dashboard, her heart pounding.

The gravity of her actions hit her like a wave. She had always convinced herself that her choices were justified, that she had been wronged, and this was her way of taking control. But now, sitting alone in the dark, there was no one left to lie to. The truth was undeniable.

She had hurt so many people.

The memories came flooding back, all at once, as if the years of lies, manipulation, and darkness had been waiting for this exact moment to unravel.

She thought of the high school boy—the first. He had been kind to her at first, pretending to like her, leading her on. And when he left her for someone else, her jealousy had consumed her. She hadn't been able to stand the thought of him with his girlfriend, laughing, holding hands, going to prom together while she sat in the shadows. That's when she turned to witchcraft, her grandmother's old books, the rituals she barely understood but had used, nonetheless.

The accident she caused had been no accident at all. They had been on their way to prom when it happened. Their car careened off the road, and no one ever questioned how it was possible. Just another tragic teenage story, people said.

But Tabitha knew.

She closed her eyes, pressing her hands to her temples as the weight of her guilt settled deeper in her chest. And then there was Jerrimi, her husband, the man she had trapped into being with her. He had never truly loved her, not the way she had wanted. She had manipulated him, used magic to make sure he stayed with her and sealed their fate when she got pregnant with their son. But even that hadn't been enough to fill the emptiness inside her.

And then... the accident.

She had caused that too. Jerrimi had found the box. The one with the newspaper clippings, the mementos, and the proof that linked her to the deaths of the high school couple. He had confronted her about it just before he and their son left for Texas. She knew he was going to expose her, that he couldn't live with the truth. So, she made sure he never had the chance.

A tear slid down her cheek as the memory of that night came crashing back. She had told herself it was necessary, that she was protecting herself. But the truth was, she had been driven by fear—fear that her perfect life would unravel, that she would lose control.

And now, Morghan.

Morghan had been nothing but a good friend to her. She had shown her kindness and had trusted her when they met at the grief group. But Tabitha's jealousy had poisoned everything. She had seen the love between Brian and Morghan, the kind of love she had always wanted but could never have. The love that Jerrimi had never given her, not even with all the magic in the world.

She had wanted Brian for herself, convinced that if she could take Morghan's place, she would finally be happy.

But all she had done was make Morghan sick—destroying the one true friendship she had ever known. And for what?

Tabitha's hands shook as she wiped the tears from her face, her breath catching in her throat. The weight of everything she had done—the lives she had taken, the people she had hurt—crushed her.

She wanted to scream, to undo everything, but it was too late. The damage had been done.

For the first time in her life, she was truly regretful.

Sitting there in her car, Tabitha realized that all the magic, all the manipulation, had never brought her happiness. All it had brought her was pain—pain she had spread to everyone around her. And now, it was too much to bear.

She took a deep breath, forcing herself to steady. She had to face the truth. She couldn't run from it anymore.

With a shaking hand, Tabitha pulled the door handle and stepped out of the car. The hospital loomed ahead of her, and as she walked back inside, a pit formed in her stomach. She didn't know what she would say, didn't know how to make things right, but she had to try. She had to apologize, to confess. She owed that much to Brian and Morghan—at the very least.

As she approached the hallway where Morghan's room was, Tabitha's steps slowed. The fluorescent lights overhead buzzed quietly, and her heart pounded in her chest. She could see Brian through the small window in the door, sitting beside Morghan, his head bowed. The sight of them together, their bond unbroken despite everything, made her heart ache with regret.

But before she could take another step, a voice cut through her thoughts.

"Tabitha."

She turned sharply and saw Claudette standing a few feet away, her eyes narrowing as she took in the sight of her. Claudette's face was filled with a mix of anger and disgust, her lips pressing into a thin line.

"What are you doing here?" Claudette demanded, her voice low but sharp.

"I... I came to apologize," Tabitha stammered, her voice trembling. "I need to make things right. I've done horrible things, and I—"

Claudette cut her off, stepping closer. "You think you can just walk in here and apologize? After everything you've done. You nearly killed Morghan, Tabitha. You don't get to just 'make things right.'"

Tabitha swallowed, the guilt nearly choking her. "I know. I know I can't undo it, but I have to try. Please, Claudette, I'm so sorry."

Claudette's eyes focused angrily on Tabitha. "Sorry won't fix what you've done. You don't belong here."

With a swift motion, Claudette turned toward the nurse's station. "Call security," she said firmly to the nurse on duty. "Now."

The nurse hesitated for a moment before picking up the phone, her eyes darting between Claudette and Tabitha.

Tabitha's heart sank, and she knew there was no going back now. She had come to apologize, to confess, but no one would believe her—not after everything. As the nurse spoke quietly into the phone, Tabitha took a step back, her eyes filling with tears.

Claudette turned back to her, her expression cold. "You're not getting anywhere near Morghan. Not after what you've done."

Tabitha opened her mouth to speak, but the words wouldn't come. All she could do was stand there, her chest tightening with the weight of her regret. She had come to make amends, but it was too late.

Brian stood quickly, his pulse speeding. He stepped outside the room after hearing the commotion. He was immediately met with the sight of Claudette standing in the hallway, her body tense, eyes locked on Tabitha, who stood just a few feet away. Tabitha looked worn, her face pale and drawn, but there was no mistaking the fear in her eyes.

"Tabitha, what are you doing here?" Brian's voice was tight, disbelief and anger battling for control as he took in the scene before him.

Tabitha looked at him, her lips parting as if she were about to speak, but no words came out. Claudette, however, didn't hesitate.

"She was trying to come into Morghan's room," Claudette snapped, her voice sharp. "After everything she's done—she has no business being here, Brian. I told the nurse to call security."

As if on cue, two police officers appeared, quickly moving toward Tabitha, their expressions serious. One of them spoke to Claudette briefly, nodding as she explained what had happened, but Brian barely heard the exchange. His eyes were locked on Tabitha.

She didn't fight as the cops approached her, her shoulders slumped in defeat. For the first time, Brian saw something he hadn't expected in her, regret. She looked broken as if the weight of everything she'd done had finally caught up with her.

"Brian..." Tabitha's voice was barely a whisper, but he heard it clearly. "I'm so sorry."

Brian's chest tightened, a flood of emotions rising within him. He wanted to lash out, to tell her how much pain she had caused, how close she had come to destroying his family. But as he looked at her, all he saw was a woman consumed by her own demons—someone who had lost herself in a desperate plea for something that had never been hers to begin with.

"I never meant for it to go this far," Tabitha continued, her voice shaking. "I—" She choked on her words, tears brimming in her eyes. "I was wrong about everything. I just wanted... I wanted what you and Morghan have. But I know now I can't have it. I'm sorry for what I did to her. For what I did to all of you."

Brian stood still, his fists clenched at his sides as the words washed over him. He glanced at Claudette, who was watching the scene with steady eyes, then back at Tabitha. His heart was pounding, but as much as he wanted to hate her, all he could feel was pity.

He took a slow step toward her, his voice low and calm but firm. "Tabitha, I hope you get the help you need. But you need to understand this: whatever you were looking for, whatever you thought you could take from us, it's over."

Tabitha's eyes blinked, and a single tear slid down her cheek.

"I don't know what's broken inside of you," Brian continued, "but you can't fix it by hurting other people. I hope you find peace, but you're never going to find it here. Never contact Morghan again. Do you understand me?"

Tabitha swallowed hard, her gaze dropping to the floor as she nodded slowly.

"I'm sorry," she whispered again, barely audible.

Before Brian could respond, one of the officers stepped forward. "Ma'am, you're under arrest for the attempted murder of Morghan Alexander."

Tabitha didn't resist. She allowed them to take her by the arm, her head bowed in defeat. As they led her down the hallway, Brian watched her go, a strange mix of relief and sorrow settling in his chest.

Claudette let out a long breath, her posture relaxing as she turned to Brian. "I wasn't going to let her get anywhere near Morghan," she said quietly.

Brian nodded, his eyes still on the spot where Tabitha had stood. "I know."

There was a long silence between them before Claudette spoke again, her voice softer now. "Do you think she meant it? The apology?"

Brian let out a slow breath, shaking his head. "I don't know. Maybe she did. But it doesn't matter now. She's gone."

Claudette nodded, relief washing over her face. "Good."

Brian glanced back at the door to Morghan's room, his heart aching with the weight of everything that had happened. But as he turned back to Claudette, his expression softened. "Thank you. For everything. I don't know what we would've done without you."

Claudette smiled faintly, reaching out to hug him. "You don't have to thank me, Brian. I'd do anything for you and Morghan."

Brian nodded, his gaze drifting back toward the hallway where Tabitha had disappeared. The darkness she had brought into their lives was finally starting to lift, but he knew the road ahead would still be difficult. Some scars couldn't be erased, wounds that would take time to heal.

But as he stepped back into the room, where Morghan lay resting, Brian felt something he hadn't felt in days: hope.

Chapter Twenty-Seven
A New Day

The next day, inside the hospital room, Brian sat at Morghan's bedside, holding her hand, the tension that had gripped him for days beginning to ease. Erich sat in another chair not far across the room. Morghan's color had slowly returned, her breathing more even, and for the first time in what felt like an eternity, her eyes fluttered open.

"Brian?" she whispered, her voice hoarse but steady.

Brian's heart leaped in his chest. He leaned forward, his grip on her hand tightening gently. "Morghan... I'm here. You're going to be okay."

Morghan blinked, her eyes adjusting to the bright hospital lights. She smiled faintly, her face softening as she looked at him. "What happened? I feel... different."

Brian swallowed hard, his emotions catching in his throat. "You've been sick, really sick. But you're getting better now. The doctors think you're going to be okay."

As if on cue, the door to the room opened, and a nurse stepped in, followed by the doctor who had been overseeing

Morghan's care. Both of them wore relieved expressions, the tension that had hung over the hospital staff for days finally beginning to lift.

"I'll let you guys talk," Erich said as he excused himself from the room.

"How are you feeling, Morghan?" the doctor asked, checking her vitals as he spoke.

Morghan blinked, her mind still a little foggy, but she nodded. "I feel... better. Tired, but better."

The doctor smiled. "That's a good sign. Your body is responding well to the treatments, and we're hopeful for a full recovery. There's just one more thing we need to discuss."

Brian's brow lifted, his grip on Morghan's hand tightening slightly. "What is it?"

The doctor exchanged a glance with the nurse before turning back to Morghan and Brian, his smile widening. "It seems we've discovered something else during your tests, Morghan. Congratulations, you're pregnant."

The room went still for a moment as the words hung in the air. Morghan's eyes widened in surprise, and Brian's mouth fell open in shock.

"Pregnant?" Morghan whispered, her hand instinctively moving to her stomach. "Are you sure?"

The doctor nodded. "Yes. It's still very early, but you're definitely expecting. It looks like you and Brian are going to have a baby."

Tears welled up in Brian's eyes as he looked at Morghan, his heart swelling with love and relief. After everything they had been through, the grief, the pain, the fear, this was the miracle they hadn't even dared to pray for.

"I can't believe it," Brian said softly, his voice thick with emotion. "We're going to have another baby."

Morghan smiled through her own tears, squeezing Brian's hand. "We are."

As the soft hum of the hospital machines filled the room, Brian leaned down, pressing a gentle kiss to Morghan's forehead. "We're going to be okay," he whispered, his heart full of love and hope. "We're going to be more than okay."

EPILOGUE:
Two Years Later

The warm afternoon sun poured through the floor-to-ceiling windows of the Alexander's home, casting a beautiful glow over the living room. Laughter rang through the house as little BJ, nearly three years old, ran around with his toy truck, his giggles filling the space with an innocence that Morghan cherished.

She watched him for a moment before shifting her gaze to the unopened envelopes on the coffee table. The familiar handwriting sent a shiver down her spine. Another letter.

She sighed, pressing her fingers against her temples before finally picking it up. She had kept this secret for months, but she couldn't anymore.

"Brian, we need to talk," she called out.

Her husband appeared from the kitchen, wiping his hands on a dish towel. "What's up, babe?"

Morghan hesitated, then handed him the letter. His jaw tensed as he scanned the envelope. "What's this?" He replied starring at the envelope. Morghan didn't respond right away as she walked towards the bedroom to retrieve the box. She handed Brian the box.

"They've been coming for months now."

Brian's closed his eyes in frustration. "And you didn't tell me?"

"I didn't know how," she said softly. "I wasn't sure how I felt about it. But…I need closure, Brian. I need to see her. One last time."

Brian shook his head, tossing the letter onto the table. "Closure? It's been two years, Morghan. We have moved on, we've forgiven her. She doesn't deserve space in our lives anymore."

"I know. But this isn't just about her. It's about me too."

His shoulders tensed, his lips pressed into a hard line. "I don't like this. Not one bit."

Morghan stepped closer, cupping his face in her hands. "I hear you, babe. But I have to do this."

Brian exhaled sharply, frustration in his eyes. "And if she tries to manipulate you?"

"I'm not who I was when I met her. I'm at peace," Morghan replied.

After a long moment, he nodded reluctantly. "Fine. But after this, it's over. No more letters. No more Tabitha."

"Agreed," Morghan said.

The Next Morning - Crestwood Correctional Facility

The sterile walls and fluorescent lights of the prison visitation room were suffocating. Morghan sat stiffly in the metal chair, her fingers interlaced in her lap as she waited.

Then, the heavy door creaked open.

Tabitha McClain stepped inside, wearing the standard orange jumpsuit. Her once meticulously styled hair was now pulled back into a tight ponytail, and the dark circles beneath her eyes hinted at sleepless nights.

For a moment, neither of them spoke. Then, Tabitha offered a weak, hesitant smile.

"You look good, Morghan," she said, her voice softer than Morghan remembered.

Morghan didn't return the sentiment. "Now that I'm here, Tabitha what would you like to say?"

Tabitha swallowed hard and sat down across from her. "Because I needed to tell you I'm sorry. Face to face."

Morghan kept her expression unreadable. "You've been saying that in your letters for months."

"I know," Tabitha admitted, shifting uncomfortably. "But I needed you to really hear it. I wasn't in my right mind back then. I let jealousy and resentment eat me alive. I let my own pain justify something that was unforgivable."

She blinked back tears, her voice cracking. "I hate who I was. And I hate what I did to you. You were my close friend, Morghan. And I tried to" she broke off, shaking her head. "I deserve to be here. Every single day, I wake up knowing that. But I just… I needed you to know that I don't expect anything from you. I just needed you to know how deeply sorry I am."

For the first time, Morghan saw something in Tabitha's eyes she hadn't ever seen. Regret. True regret.

Morghan let out a slow breath. "I believe you."

Tabitha's eyes widened slightly, almost as if she hadn't expected to hear that.

"And I forgive you," Morghan continued.

A tear slipped down Tabitha's cheek. "You do?"

"Yes," Morghan said, her voice steady. "Now forgive yourself". But understand this, this is the last time we will ever speak. You will not write to me. You will not reach out to Brian. This is over, Tabitha. We are done." I pray you find peace and healing in the 10 years you have left here.

Tabitha nodded, her lips trembling. "I understand."

Morghan studied her for a moment longer, then stood up.

Without another word, she turned and walked toward the exit.

As she stepped outside into the sunlight, she inhaled deeply, as if releasing the last remnants of her past with Tabitha. She pulled her sunglasses from her purse, slid them onto her face, and strode toward her car.

Sliding into the driver's seat, she took one last glance at the looming prison walls in her rearview mirror. Then, with a quiet resolve, she started the engine, pulled onto the highway, and never looked back.

The past was finally behind her.